Where the Heart is
and
Dreamscapes

Other titles by the author:

Yoga Pocket Teacher. London: Transworld, 1968.

Basic Biosciences. Sydney: McClelland, 1976.

Your Health: Vitamins and Minerals. Sydney: Doubleday, 1982.

Your Lifestyle: Health and Nutrition. Sydney: Doubleday, 1984.

Modern Naturopathy. Sydney: Harper & Row, 1986.

The Book of Relaxation. Sydney: Simon & Schuster, 1988.

Diary of a Dropout. Sydney: Wellspring, 1990.

A Spirituality for the 21st Century. Zeus, 2008

Gone Bush. Xlibris 2009

Where the Heart is

and

Dreamscapes

Short stories with a theme

*"The only place that can really be called home
is the place is it impossible to leave."*

Russell Frank Atkinson

ISBN: 978-09945919-7-5 (pbk)
eISBN: 978-0-9945919-9-9

CONTENTS

Where the Heart Is

Dreamscapes

CLEO

Sydney 1968

Andy had spent a lot of money getting his new studio together, because no other photographer had a studio you could drive into. Andy thought this would put him on the map big time. To launch another career so far from London he decided to have a grand opening. He invited the top Art Directors, Account Executives, their assistants and leading models to a Vicar and Tarts party. Smart move, Andy. They loved the idea and turned up en masse. That night was an eventful one for the business. Top executives changed companies, new ideas were invented and friendships forged and forgotten. It caused many giant hangovers. And I met Cleo, damn it.

I went with a few chaps from my outfit and lost them in the first few minutes, off hunting. Andy and I sat in the office having a few snorts and waiting for that moment when the critical mass burgeoned into a blast. It happened early. I had just downed my second Campari when we heard the volume go up and The Village People belt out 'YMCA'. In no time the joint was jumping so we downed drinks and went to where the action was. It was a merry old sight. The studio dolly, the lights, spots, props and reflectors were standing neatly in one corner of the huge space. In the other Andy had positioned a big projecting spotlight I had lent him. This device winds a wide roll of transparent film from one side to another and back again, designed to project moving images onto a rear projection screen. We had painted the film with psychedelic patterns in brilliant colours that now swirled over the Tarts and Vicars, Cardinals, Priests, Ministers, and Bishops. The walls seemed to be as alive with movement and colour as the floor.

It was one of those balmy spring nights when even ordinary places seem to promise something: something important maybe. Something you desired. Some wonder seemed close enough to touch, even though it was so nebulous it was not possible to know. And here were the beautiful people having fun. All the men seemed handsome, the women beautiful. Those walking past could feel the lightness, the joy of living effused by this merry throng of successful people and hung about the footpath wistfully looking in.

I sharpened the focus on the spotlight and hid in its shadow to enjoy the view. Up on a chair I could see it all, even the dim figures of the spectators out in the street. Groups were standing about, their backs screens for the projected images as they picked finger foods from the buffet tables. Others talked in small groups or sat in director's chairs looking on, but most of them were dancing alone, or with a partner or two. I saw a red Bishop complete with crosier doing a steamy fandango with a scarlet woman in a slinky dress, a red handbag bouncing about her crooked elbow. Other Tarts wore net stockings, mini skirts and halters; high-heeled shoes kicked off, gyrating dizzily. Some ecclesiastical gentlemen with great eclat danced now with one, now with another sexy Tart advertising her attractions one way or another. Sally, an old girlfriend of mine, had got it down to suspenders knickers and bra. (Typical.) A celebrant, robed and mitred, walked with a stately gait swinging a censer. The studio smelt like St. Mary's Cathedral on Christmas morning mixed with the back bar of the Bognor on Friday nights. A synod of Cardinals was convened about a bevy of slinky beauties tempting them from the straight and narrow with lewd remarks I had no doubt. I saw Andy sneak into his office with the gorgeous Gail in tow. The horns of the Tijuana Brass were blasting the paint off the walls.

Anya sailed past, slid to a halt and said "What in the hell are you doing skulking in the corner?" grabbed me and whisked me off into the foray. Half an hour later I staggered into Andy's office where I had secreted a few bottles of my favorite Shiraz. Andy and Gail had decamped so I sat and quaffed a glass and carrying another, went to sample the canapés and hors-d'oeuvres. By this time I was in the mood for convivial conversation. I chatted up a few tipsy tarts and while circulating bumped into Andy who introduced me to a slick little wench, a friend of Gail's. I took a fancy to her and decided to get ambitious. Off we danced to some slinky numbers from the Manhattan Transfer. We stopped twisting and gyrating slowing to a friendly clinch in quarter time. Things were looking good.

"What are you drinking?" I asked.

"The last one was Cinzano on the rocks with a twist."

"Fancy a top red?"

"Lead me to it!"

"Great! Step this way." I took her hand and made through the crowd towards the office but a drunken Conga line intercepted us. I felt her hand slip from mine and when I stood at the office door looking for her she was nowhere to be seen. Tipsy by now I muttered 'easy come easy go' and downed another red.

Shortly after midnight, I was no longer a participant but a rather abstracted observer - the effect of dancing, rich food and a bottle and a half of Angel's Blood. Those on their feet were shuffling about to romantic ballads from Harper's Bazaar, either cheek to cheek or cheek to chest. Small groups sat talking shop, others had heads together singing an Aussie folk song. A Bishop, excommunicated, sat propped up by the wall, his tall mitred hat askew over an ear and his crosier leaning against his sleeping head. Two Tarts were standing next to me, backs against the wall looking on. I heard the neat little number say to her tall blond friend in a tone that held some pique, "Well then, I'm going home!" As she moved past me I felt like a person in the back seat of a car watching a driver in the front seat do the driving. I watched while that other person stepped forward and said something like, "But you can't do that now! How will we ever meet if you go?"

She looked back at her friend who was following her, laughed, held out her hand and said "Cleo." The driver took her hand and shook it warmly and said "Cedric Reginald Bartram. Friends and lovers call me Bart". "Or Ram?" she said. That's how it started.

Do beginnings determine ends I wonder? Glib repartee became our trademark, mine with whimsy usually, Cleo's acerbic, often spiteful. So much of the time I felt driven; just a back-seat observer. Sometimes I felt like I did not know the man behind the wheel. Thinking over that strange affair I wonder if there were actually four of us trying to come to grips with each other. There were certainly two Cleo's. She was, after all, a Gemini. One was light and witty, intelligent and perceptive. The other could appear at any time if there was company about. At those times she became a hateful witch. That Cleo never surfaced when we were alone. In fact, the alone Cleo would never acknowledge what the Cleo in company had done. She both fascinated and scared me. I got to wonder about that other woman at the party.

Cleo's expressive mouth intrigued me. I loved to watch it when she was in animated conversation. It was beautifully out of proportion to the rest of her face. Her top lip was not sculptured as some are but appeared to be almost a gentle arc above the full lower lip. There were small depressions where they met. When she smiled they disappeared and the red arc dipped down in the center. It was most beguiling. After a time it became possible for me to gauge her innermost feelings by the way those most expressive lips moved. They became, along with certain words, a signal that a metamorphosis was likely. Whenever I heard her announce that she was going home or the word was used in some other context and the lips hardened into a tight sort of pout, I knew what would follow. Lacking courage towards the end, I would head for home myself.

About a year after the party Andy asked, "What's with this Cleo bird? She some sort of nut? The way she gave it to you the other night I don't know why you bother with her. Christ! She must be good in bed is that it?" I would have liked it to be that simple. There was next to no sexual attraction for me. Yet we were passionate about each other. Strange, isn't it?

Often, I tried to let it simmer out but then would come this plaintive phone call I couldn't resist. Twice I took the wheel and broke it off. Then she would start appearing at my usual haunts, often with the tall blond. There she would be! - dining with some bloke at my favorite restaurant or sun baking on my favorite rock by the harbor pool. 'Severe withdrawal symptoms,' she would say. I tried to resist from the back seat but that fool at the wheel drove me on. It was such great fun to get back together again – for a time anyway.

But I could not keep going in this way and made some dishonest and cowardly excuses. How could I ever forget the last time I saw her? I had not seen her to talk to for months and wondered, a little hurt, why she had not tried to contact me as she usually did. She phoned early one Saturday morning. "I must see you," she said. "I need to clear my head so I'm going up to the headland for a while. See you there in a half-hour, OK?" Surprised, I was about to mumble some excuses but she hung up. The man in the back seat cried 'Don't go!' but the weak fool in the front seat could not hear. 'I can't just leave the girl waiting up there alone. What else can I do?' he said. So we both went.

My heart sank when I saw her, looking disheveled. My heart sank further when I saw her lips. I was about to give her a friendly peck on the cheek but she started to berate me with the last words I had spoken to her months before.

"I remember what you said perfectly well," Cleo said. I caught a glimpse of the familiar sideways glance from those splendid eyes, though I was gazing out over the sluggish waters of the harbor. "...Perfectly well..." Cleo said.

I felt rather than saw, that sideways glance again, detecting the intimations of scorn, perhaps even of malice.

"Look," I said, growing impatient with her attitude of omniscience, "I was there too, remember? What I said was I just couldn't go on like that any longer. It wasn't because I didn't love you. Couldn't you see that I was swamped – out of my depth?"

"Now I suppose you are going to tell me you said what you did because you loved me too much ... overwhelmed with passion or some such romantic nonsense," she said, walking to the railing and looking down pensively onto the rocks far below. A breeze from the sea blew a long strand of hair across her eyes. She flicked it back over an ear with a quick impatient gesture.

"Good God!" I wailed, "Don't you remember that that was exactly what I did say? I didn't want to lose you but I just couldn't go on! How could you forget!"

She turned in fury, eyes ablaze.

"I remember! I remember!" she screamed. Her handbag hit me in the face, dazing me. All the letters I had sent her fell out and blew about. As I was hastening to gather them up I heard her laugh. I looked up the very instant she leaped over the rail: dress billowing ... hair flying, screaming out, "I'm going home!" It haunts me even now.

THE WAY BACK HOME

A Dog's Tale. Sydney – Hampton 1935

We all took the move to the city pretty well, considering. Surprisingly, little Julie, our youngest, took it in her stride. Came home from Kindy all agog with new things to do and so many kids to play with. Young Tommy was out of sorts for a few months and hung about the house fiddling with his Mechano set and building blocks and didn't want to go out much. He was OK after he met Mike from down the street and started playing cricket with his brothers in their back yard.

Pam and I were like fish out of water for a long time, but we adjusted. The only member of the family who couldn't cope was old Ranger. Some of the neighbours found coping with Ranger was a problem. They had never seen a real dog. Part Irish Deer hound, he stood knee high to me and I'm not short. He was deep chested with lean hind quarters, long legged, large and hairy. His bark scared the living daylights out of postmen and hawkers even if Ranger was out of sight. Posties made sure the gate was closed and salesmen bolted for it when Ranger came around the corner of the house. There were a few complaints.

They didn't know that he was a noble soul. Thinking of him now it is possible, for the first time, to realize that we never thought of him as just a dog. Certainly not as a pet. He was one of us. He thought so too. When Tommy was a toddler he would walk down the paddock holding Ranger's collar and old Ranger would take small steps so that Tommy could keep up with him.

"Where's Tommy?" Pam would ask. "Out with Ranger." I would say.

That old dog knew when a roo shoot was on. He would sit outside the fly screen door barking. As soon as I came out with the 12-gauge he would run to the Dodge and sit on the running board with his fore paws up on the mud guard. He would sit there with his ears blowing back over his collar and a big grin on his face as me and the blokes drove into the hills. Sometimes, coming back at sunset a roo would be startled on the road side and take off into the scrub. We might be doing fifty, but that dog would leap off the car and take off after it. We used to wait a while but if he didn't show after a half hour or so, we would go home. Ranger would turn up a day or so later as if he just been down the dam for a swim. No matter where we were when he took off he always found his way back home.

He knew so much, that dog. Back in '29 I had the only butcher shop in town, on Ridge road. There was a gully behind, where I used to park the car. I cut a few steps in the clay to get up and down. Most days Ranger would ride in with me and poke about all day and I would chuck some trimmings out to him. There were a lot of dead-beats about in those years and lots of people had to run up big accounts, but I didn't fret them much. I reckoned we were better off than most, with the shop and a milch cow. Anyhow, some took matters into their own hands sometimes. One Friday night after I did the till and closed up I put the takings – about a hundred quid or so – into my Gladstone bag, locked up and went down the gully. I opened the boot to put the bag in when one of the dead-beats jumped out from behind a tree and grabbed it. Ranger leapt at him and pinned the poor bastard to the ground. All he could see was a great hairy head and a mouth full of fangs. Boy! Did that bloke looked scared! As if his last day had come. After I called Ranger off, I gave the hard-up five bob and told him to make himself scarce.

After he had settled down a bit and stopped prowling around being cranky, Pam took him shopping with her. He didn't like the lead but being Ranger, behaved himself. People stopped to ask what sort of a dog it was, standing off. Others thought there was nothing a dog liked better than having his head patted and his ears fondled. Ranger let them know otherwise. He would shake his head, look insulted and give a little growl. Nobody did it twice.

Pam left him sitting head high and looking very dignified outside the grocer shop. The old dog leaned forward to give a passing child a friendly lick, but the child ran screaming to his mother. His mother went off the rails. When Pam came out of the shop she got a tongue lashing and was told she must be mad to bring a wolf out on the streets and that she was going to report it to the police, the RSPCA, the Zoo and the Prime Minister. Pam was upset of course, so without telling the kids until after the deed was done, we decided that the best thing to do was to take Ranger back to the farm.

Early one morning. I put the old boy on the back seat for a change and made off to the farm over on the western slopes. Bernie, the lay-about, got a big surprise when I drove up to his hut by the creek. Ranger jumped out, glad to be back, gave Bernie a lick and romped around with his mate Bluey the cattle dog. I hadn't seen him so full of beans for a long time.

"What brings you back Clarry" Bernie asked.

"Well, time I looked the place over I reckon, but the real reason is the old dog. He's not a city dog is he? Reckon he's better off with you and Bluey."

"Well, I told you that before you went didn't I? Its OK with Bluey and me but he's going to be sore as hell when you take off and leave him."

"Yeah, nothing surer. I know you'll both hate it, but keep him chained up a few days so he doesn't take off after me. Let him settle in for a bit to get used to the idea. Keep him close by and maybe in the hut of nights."

My God it was hard to say goodbye to that dog. He knew soon as the chain was clipped onto his collar. The way he looked at me, woebegone but without blame, accusing but without rancour, just about broke my heart. I hugged him and strode to the car, waving to Bernie so he couldn't see my eyes were so watery that I could hardly see to drive.

Because I am a family person, as are all of my kind, home is wherever the family are. I was glad to be back because this was our home and I felt that the rest of them would be here too, before long. When He was talking to Bernie I got a whiff of reluctance and sadness but I didn't know that it was about me. But I knew as soon as He clipped that chain on my collar. I pleaded with Him not to do it. I saw that He knew what I was feeling and I could smell the sadness coming out of Him and that made me feel a bit better about it. Then He got into the car and drove off. Back to the rest of the pack, I felt. But why didn't He take me with Him? I couldn't understand it.

I felt very lost and sad for a long time and Bernie and Bluey were very good. Bluey used to curl up with me the first few days. Bernie always smelt friendly anyway, of pipe tobacco and wood smoke and let me in the hut of nights, but not without the chain.

Then the lads from down the valley came to help Bernie and Bluey get the strays from off the high paddocks back. They thought I was a working dog and let me off the chain. Bernie smelt of anxious worry and had a few hard words to say.

I pretended I would help and trotted alongside Bernie's horse for a while, but when they got to the scrub I let them get ahead and then ran back as fast as I could and ate the rest of the rabbit Bernie had thrown me and whatever Bluey had left, took a big drink from the trough and made off down the valley road. I knew that the dirt road met a black one and that the black one went all over the place in a big curve, so when I got to it I took a rest and felt about where I was and where they would be. The sun was still low in the sky and that was the direction I had to take, so I went towards it into the hills.

By the time the sun was going down I was tired, hungry, and thirsty. I smelt some old water and found it in a stump. I rested to lick my paws and dozed off for a while. I heard dogs howling in the dark. The ones who lived here before we lot came. I trotted on until their scent was strong so I stopped to sniff. One of them was wanting a mate and I got carried away by urgency, so when I came across her tracks I followed them to an overhang where she was. She was teasing the others, snapping at one end and smelling enticing at the other, but when I showed up they ignored her and rushed snarling and barking at me. I stood my ground and showed them my teeth which stopped them in their tracks. They began to sidle around me, so one of them could get behind and bite me where it hurts most. I waited, moving slowly towards the rocks. I let the youngest get behind me and as soon as I felt his move, I wheeled, bit his ear and rolled him, yelling, to the ground. I slashed his neck and leapt up against the rocks growling fiercely. Three slunk off smelling of surrender, but the big one turned and came back, smelling angry, staring into my eyes. I met the challenge by rushing him and showing all my fangs which made his look like prickles. He slunk off, head down, tail between his legs.

She came to me right away. We joined our breath and smelt our parts and knew that a mix was needed. We played around a bit. She took me to her cache where there was some wombat. We ate together. I was very grateful for that food though the taste was strange. She was uncomfortable so she started rubbing it against me and with a rush of blood I mounted her and she whimpered in satisfaction as I swelled up inside her. We were enjoying it like that when the big dog came sniffing around. I couldn't let him get behind me so I had to turn so she and I were tail to tail. I went for him dragging her backwards behind me. He kept well away, but sat down, watching and waiting. He waited a long time. Later, we chased him off.

I learnt a lot from her the next few days. Things I had no idea about – that yabbies in the creek could be caught and that cicadas, frogs and water dragons made good rich food and that even the spiny anteater could be eaten if you knew how to go about it. But the family were somewhere else so I had to go. Early one morning I sniffed all directions and headed, once again, for home.

After the wooded hills there were paddocks with many cows all standing facing me and eyeing me steadily as I loped past. Sometimes, just for fun, I would rush at them and bark and the fools would panic and rush off in all directions.

One night I heard dogs barking not far off. I had not eaten for a while and was thirsty too, so I rolled in a cow pat so I smelt of cow and went to investigate. I was drinking at the tank when I heard a growl. I said a friendly yap and waited to see what came next. A sheep dog came out from under the tank stand and we sniffed each other. He was a youngster who had not mated yet. He felt that I was something special. I felt that I was too, compared to a young sheep dog who had never sown his seed and not even hunted a bandicoot, let alone a wallaby. He felt special too, because he could take me to meet the others. They were all good working dogs. They wanted to hear about all my adventures. I took them down to the creek to show them about frogs and yabbies and they were very impressed.

It was slaughter day so there was food aplenty, so I stayed on, filling up and resting. I hid in the old shack where the homestead used to be and the others came down of nights for a romp. It was a good time, but my family were not here, so I had to go. They all came down to the timber to see me off. Young Butch wanted to come too, feeling for some adventure. I was relieved when the top dog put him in his place for forgetting his duty to the boss and the others, which made him feel his youth and inexperience.

A few more suns brought me down the slopes and things got a bit easier and a bit harder. The farms were smaller with a lot of row crops and the country was flatter but with lots more fences. Some bit when I touched them. There was more food to be scrounged instead of hunted, but it could be dangerous. Twice I was shot at. I have a hole through one ear as a result.

Then a funny thing happened. I was caught trying to get out of a chicken run. I got in all right but the chooks woke up and started a flutter and a squawk that set the dogs barking. A drum fell over the hole I had dug and I couldn't get out. In no time out came the farmer with a his shot gun. He must have spotted my collar. He slung the gun over his arm and came to take a good look. Then he yelled out and after a while, two sleepy looking blokes and an old woman came out of the house. They all smelt strange. There were lots of different smells. They stood about talking a lot. The chooks were clucking in a huddle up the other end of the run. I tried to look friendly and harmless. The old man came up to the wire talking to me all the time. The old woman went back inside. The old man made all those sounds they make to us and he smelt all right so when he opened the door I came out and went to him grinning and wagging my tail like it would spin off. He spat on his palm and rubbed it on my nose. He knew about us, that old man. Lots of farmers smell a bit like him. I liked him right off. He looked at my nose, paws and eyes, at the holed ear and looked under my tail. He gave some instructions and the two younger men went off. The old man kept talking to me softly while he took some burrs out of my coat and took a good look at my collar. The two men came back, each with a Greyhound on a lead. They looked at me as if I was cat shit. I've never met such a stuck-up pair since I was a pup. They smelt of chemicals like sheep dip and treated me like I wasn't even a dog.

The old man was all right, though he smelt sour and unhappy a lot of the time. The woman did too, but there was the sickly sweet smell of the disease that meant she didn't have long to live. Maybe that was what made the old man sad. Their sons were full of snarls and unnatural smells, just like those snooty dogs, so after a few days scrounging whatever I could and resting up, I made off home again.

The going got harder and harder, with more streets, houses and cars that scared me. Some evenings I could smell the tang of the sea and knew I must be getting closer to home. For a while I was sure I was lost. There were so many strong and different smells that I got confused and didn't know where to go. I found a park and moped around for few days eating scraps from garbage bins until a man in a truck came and tried to throw a net over me, so I ran off and walked through the streets as far as I could, until I had to rest. When I woke up there was a different feel. I went round in circles slowly a few times, feeling for Him and the rest of the pack and sniffing for hints. One direction made a tingle inside my head. I went that way and walked all night. Apart from meeting a few dogs and lots of cats it was a lot quieter at night, without the noise and smell of the cars and trucks that I couldn't get used to. The next day I hid and started out after dark. The following day the place felt a lot like where they all were - stenches everywhere and no breezes to blow them away or bring interesting smells. I could never understand why they came to such a place. I wandered around, scrounging about for many suns. I was thin, sick, lonely and weak. I felt that I wouldn't last too much longer. I was a sad, lost dog.

One day, I found a park, which was a blessing, so stayed there to rest. Some children came to play cricket there and I caught an old familiar smell. I couldn't believe my nose. I rushed over to the boys and there he was – Tommy! I slobbered in joy and licked his face in relief.

Tommy jumped with joy too, and after hugging me and asking wherever I had been, he took me home.

ॐ

About two weeks after I had left Ranger chained up, Bernie phoned from the post office to say that Ranger had gone. It upset Pam, but I told her not to fret, he had probably gone off to visit some of his mates down the valley, or maybe Thompson's big bitch had come on heat like happened a few years ago. She said yes, maybe, and left it at that. A month or so later Bernie phoned again to say that Ranger was still missing and that no one down the valley had sighted him since the day we left. We didn't tell the kids.

It clouded our minds a lot and we told ourselves all sorts of notions, but the time came when we had to admit that we would never see the grand old dog again. Pam and I talked about what sort of lies we would tell Julie and Tommy, when, blow me down! Young Tommy came home one afternoon with Ranger, like always. You could have knocked Pam down with a feather. She gave him the T-bone steak she had for my dinner and some of the kid's chops and they all just about hugged old Ranger to death. When I got home the old dog heard the gate click and came bounding down the path wagging from the tip of his nose to the end of his tail and bounded about my legs so much I couldn't walk. I'm not too proud to admit that I went in to wash the tears off my face.

You mightn't believe the story but it's true. That dog walked all the way from the western slopes, over the Blue Mountains, across the plains to the western suburbs and through suburb after suburb and over the Lane Cove river until he found us. He's the truest friend a man ever had.

FULL OF GRACE

I always loved my son in spite of the way he treated me. But that is just like a mother isn't it? He was such a beautiful baby. He was chubby and radiant and a joy to everybody at first. He was merry and mischievous. He was so naughty! But in such a sweet way that I would have to give him a hug instead of a slap.

But as he got older Joe and I became worried about him. I don't suppose there was anything to worry about really, because he was very bright but he didn't play with the other children but would just sit quietly sometimes all by himself. Quite happy but just sitting doing nothing! Joe and I thought he was sick; maybe in the head even, but he seemed well enough really.

Playing pranks is one thing, but it was a real worry when the Elders came to see Joe about our boy hanging about the temple all the time causing trouble. Singing louder than the Cantor. Arguing with the Rabbis even! Would you believe it? A boy of ten already! Then when Joe gave him a big scolding he just smiled and said yes dad but took to going out into the wilderness all on his own all day. Without even a cut-lunch yet! Such a worry he was. Such a worry!

Why did he neglect me so, when he was older? I ask you, who was it who worked so hard to keep him from the bad company in the slums in which we were forced to live because of Joe being so daft. Never could keep a job more than a week or two. Who was it took in laundry I am ashamed to say so my boy could be well fed? Who had him taught reading and writing and the Law? Who do you suppose sat up nights with a burning candle and sewed him shirts and knitted him shawls and yarmulkes? His father was a good man, mind, but he was so otherworldly. Aloof sort of. He didn't seem to care about those down-to earth sorts of things. Such a schlemiel he was! Should never have married I think - except that he had no choice seeing as how things turned out. Of course maybe it was my fault too. I was such a good mother so he left it all to me I suppose. Men!

Up to the time my boy left I was the apple of his eye. Such a devoted son he was. He never wanted to be with his father, only with me. It was marvelous when he made me little things from bits of wood and timber he had found or filched. He was so clever with his hands too, you know. Then when he was a young man he just up and left. Disappeared without so much as a by-your-leave even. But when he came back – fifteen years already! It was father this and father that – his mother who had bore him and did so much for him never got so much as a mention. I shouldn't be all that surprised, should I? You would think we women would have learned not to expect anything else by now wouldn't you? How we mothers suffer you wouldn't want to know. If he had only met a nice girl and married and settled down.

I was so embarrassed when he turned up again after all those years looking like a bum and saying all those terrible things like he and his father were one, and causing such a stir. I could have hidden away and pretended not to know him, but a mother is a mother and what could I do when I saw him? In spite of what I had meant to him; how I had tended to his every need and how he had doted on me, what did he do when I went to embrace my boy? – He said something like 'Woman, what have I to do with you?' – or something like that – I don't remember exactly – it was so long ago. So I should suffer so much? What a thing for a boy to say to his mother!

Another thing, he was so secretive about what he had been up to all those years. Could I find out anything about it yet? No. It was my right to an explanation don't you think? I asked his friends about it (such friends too I might say – fisher people and riffraff they were) but they were very nice I must say. Some of them treated me very special and I liked that about them, but by and large they were a pretty scruffy lot. My boy's closest friends! So well educated he was! Couldn't he do better than that? But I never did find out, so I guessed he had gone off to where ever those three weirdo's had drifted in from with that silly story when he was born.

Of course, he had heard the story from our neighbors when he was a boy and I suppose it was natural enough for an adventurous boy to go off like he did. But without telling his mother? My heart bleeds. I mean, the rumors I have heard you wouldn't believe already. His followers were a crazy lot in my opinion. But what does an old widow's opinion count? Not a sesame seed. I mean, they came up with that story about me being a virgin which I used to be of course until Joe took me for a walk in the garden of Gethsemane one spring night and wound up making a women of me.

They spread a rumor too about an angel coming to tell me that my baby was to be the Messiah! What next! The truth is I didn't know a thing about all that. All I know is that he came close to being a bastard. Joe did the right thing, though, thank God. Who would have thought that he would become famous with people fawning over him as something special? And because of all that the most terrible thing happened to him. After that I was never the same woman. There isn't a day goes by that my heart doesn't bleed at the memory of his poor skinny body hanging there. I really don't know how I have managed.

There were so many stories floating about that I didn't know if I was Zeekal or Meekal most of the time. And he didn't help with all those fibs he told either. Fancy telling everybody that he had no place to lay his head! Really! He knew very well that I had kept his room clean and tidy just like it was the day he went away and there were his tools in the box I had given him to keep them in and all his scrolls and pictures of David and Abraham and his nice little bed with its cotton sheets for summer and the lamb's wool cover for the winter. Nowhere to lay his head indeed! He knew very well that if he stopped all that Messiah nonsense that he could come home whenever he wished. So he was hanging up there along with common criminals and I cry every time I think of it. That scruffy lot that followed him have gone Jehovah knows where and here am I alone with Joe gone and all. God knows what's to become of me.

AUDA OF ARABIA

Damascus October 1st. 1918 (Armistice Day, WW1)

*(Auda abu Tayi was an Arab tribal leader who
fought the Turks under the influence of T. E Lawrence
who achieved world-wide fame as Lawrence of Arabia;
'that Englishman' in the story)*

The great Auda abu Tayi jumped upon his feet and cried,

"HO! Shall I tell thee how we crossed the dreadful Nefu in but three days and slew Turks at Ghadir el Haj?"

The Howeitat, leaning against their saddles, smoking or chewing leathery sun dried strips of camel meat; dreaming of deep wells and running springs as desert Arabs do, sat up. The dozing awoke.

"By God's mercy shall we not?" Nesib bellowed, laughing. Some chuckled with delight and spat. The Howeitat leaned forward or lay on their bellies, chin in hands, eager to hear the story heard many times. Auda Tayi strode about the fire, cloak sleeves billowing to his wild gestures, his voice rising and falling; now soft as the petals of Meccan roses or harsh as stones down the serrated steeps of Wadi Itm by Akaba. Striking his chest with a clenched fist he roared,

"And we were but twelve!"

(A long pause; then softly).

"In the name of Allah, the merciful; the loving-kind, we were one Sheriff and one sheik - Auda and ten Howeitat of Tayi. Of the leaders there were Sheriff Abdulla el Feir, sheik Auda abu Tayi, Gasim el Shim and Kasim of one eye.

We had rested with the Hamt at Jebel Raal and by the beard of the Prophet their hospitality was a burden on our guts. They feasted us as was befitting, on a suckling camel-calf boiled in soured asses milk quartered undrawn and mounted in a trough of buttered rice. Then on mutton stew and boiled wheat flour and sweetmeats. Our bellies groaned. Lest we grow fat so it was that one night just before dawn Auda said 'Let us make a raid upon the Turk!' and we said 'In the name of Allah the just'. And we went. Kasim in his silks and sandals of pieced leather; Auda in white robes and red head cloth; Abdulla in his blue-black burnoose: Gasim barefoot, wore cotton but with an embroided head cloth.

Thus, we left the Sheriff's great eight-bayed tent of twenty four poles and walked past the tents of Zaal and of Fahad and of Adhub the lazy and of Rahal and of Ramied the lame, waking them as we went. 'Whither?" some asked and we said 'to raid the Turk' so they too came out from the village to the camels. The bulls were grateful we took only riding she-camels for we were as full of passion as of Hamth food and took nothing but our weapons and our fury."

His voice rose until his words were spoken with a frightening but muted intensity that stirred the bowels of us all as if full of marching ants. Auda waited, sword drawn and held aloft. The tribesmen waited. Slowly we breathed again as he spoke softly, smooth as oil flows from the lips of a calabash.

"Abdulla took Namaal his Sherari racer. Auda took big Ghazal, good for two hundred and fifty miles between waterings in summer! Gasim took his silver hilted dagger set with gems, the blade cast by that servant of Allah, Mohammed ibn Zari of Jauf.

Then Auda said, 'By my very God I have an idea!'

Ramied cried 'Woe upon us! Auda has an idea!'

Rahal said 'Woe indeed, but let us hear it for my brains itch'

Auda said 'Let us attack the Turk from out of the Nefu! No Turk would think an attack from the Nefu a credible thing!'

Zaal said 'By Allah it is so!'

Abdulla said 'Then we and the Turk shall all suffer together!'

Gasim said 'This is fine madness brothers. Let us do it'

So it was that each took the most precious and rode with the coming day mindless into the Nefu."

He began pacing again, raising and lowering his torso from the knees, tapping with his riding stick as though mounted.

"In two days hard riding we came to the fringe of the Nefu. Chanting did we ride till the flints of Wadi Shta slowed the camels down while the heat filled our heads, burnt our eyes, fired our tongues and cracked our lips open. The Nefu is barren by God! It is barren barren barren.

Auda called halt at noon and said 'Curses upon the Nefu as it is a curse to men. All bare of grazing for by God this country is barren!' And Abdulla said, 'By God it *is* barren!' And Zaal said, 'By God, you are right!'

We huddled under tents of robes propped up with our riding sticks. For hours we sat silent. The sun was searing the stones so we dare not open our eyes to the quivering air. May Allah have mercy on our souls it was hot! By the very God the heat beat down upon us.

'Rise!' croaked Abdulla through cracked lips. Fahad croaked 'Rise is it?' Auda croaked 'Let us rise for Ghadir el Haj' so we rose, beast and man groaning. We rode speechless. Nothing was heard except the plop plop of our camels feet, the creak of harness and the soft swish of tassels hour after hour into the night. At the zenith we rested and drank and mounted our groaning beasts and plodded slowly on across the Nefu swaying in our saddles, beating each other and ourselves with our riding sticks that we might stay alive. The camels picked up pace so water was near and through parted fingers we saw a shimmering blur. Praise be to Allah, our course was true for it was Jebbel Gof. But a half-day and we had reached the well of Zacrik. Man and beast drank deep and rested there together as they had suffered together.

'By the will and power of Allah the all-merciful we have crossed the Nefu in under three days'. Adhar said. Zaal said 'By the will of Allah'. And Gasim said 'By the beard of the Prophet it is so!'

At Zacrik there are thorn trees and tamarisks and our eyes rejoiced in them as did our beasts and while they fed we baked bread and slept until after midnight, then rode again to the ridge above the Hejas railway at Ghadir el Haj. There we lay shivering amongst the rocks until the light of the world came. We crouched amongst the rocks at the top of that ridge until by God, by my God, by my very God; at last the sun rose upon us!

With his light our joy was great to see the tents of the Turk and the hated flag flying over the blockhouse. Watching through glasses this Auda saw the commandant and two officers come out of that blockhouse to sit upon chairs in the early sun my brothers! By God! They sat on chairs! Auda took his great-barreled rifle and kissed it. Abdulla took his .303 rifle stolen in Wejh and kissed it. Gasim took his rifle and kissed it. Brothers, I have seen Gasim drop a running Gazelle from a galloping camel with his second shot at three hundred yards. Abdulla it is said, never fires twice at the same target and Auda is Auda. Those three licked the dust off the sights and those three adjusted the sights and nestled the barrels amongst the stones. Those three judged the wind, muttered a blessing and squeezed the triggers. The three chairs were then empty.

Kasim of one eye, Zaal, Fahad, Adhub and the others, already mounted behind us, charged down upon them screaming. Their confusion was great and by the time we were upon them many lay dead. How we fought! Sword in one hand and rifle in the other we rode them down then took to pistol and dagger till it was done and we in madness had killed them all".

Here he stopped still. He looked into the staring eyes of each man; slowly...slowly. Then he beat his fist against his chest and flourishing his sword roared,

" By the goodness of Allah, the most powerful, the just, there are no men as great as the Bedu! And of the Bedu there are no men as great as the Howeitat! And of the Howeitat there are none as great as the Tayi!'

Here he waited a while-

"And of the Tayi none so great as Auda! He is a river to his people!"

His tribesmen roared assent. Some fired joy shots at the stars crying 'By the will of Allah it is so!'

"HO! Auda showed that Englishman what this old Arab could do! Thanks be to Allah the Almighty, the ever kind, we are not as the English. Planning planning planning and in the end it all comes undone!"

Then as always Zaal pleaded to hear the rest of the story. As always Auda deferred with a depreciating gesture and sat down. He took Anise seeds from his pouch and began chewing them with a far away look like a camel chewing its cud. He hummed a favorite tune as always and as always suddenly began the tale again with a detailed list of the plunder.

"Our blood was up my brothers. Still full of the passion of battle we looted, stripped and destroyed until the sun was in the zenith by God. I have told you who received the fine mortar and pestle of granite, the steel coffee pot and cups, the fine carpets and cloth and which of us fitted the officer's tunics but it was the rifles and pistols that gave us more joy. Thirty of one and twenty of the other. And cartridges. Such a day it was! Every man was roaring and screaming and shouting as he worked. Fahad wept, crying aloud and Rameid the lame shook so much from the terror of victory that he dropped the crockery he had taken a liking to and it all broke upon the lava.

Such a morning's work by God! It was rich! Rich! Rich! Then Adhub the lazy who had gone unbeknown rode in with six pack camels and five mules! By the sons of the Prophet it was rich.

Then Auda said 'Let us begone. Let us ride towards Jefir to meet Feisel and fret the Turk from Amman to Azrak even to Damascus'. 'Let us do so' said Abdulla, descendant of the Prophet.

Azzad said 'We came as a raiding party and leave as a caravan' Gasim said 'Let us begone by God' And Fahad said 'We came from out of the Nefu. Let us begone!' So we were gone from that place but the dead were left for the carrion.

We were fifteen camels and five mules heavily laden, water-skins full and flour enough to keep us out a month and well fed at that – a camel with a bullet hole in its lip but teeth intact and a man with a through wound of no account and one of us minus an ear. But my brothers, that was many moons ago. Thanks be to Allah the just, the ever- kind, we are in Damascus now and the war is won! -. By my very God it is a marvelous thing, so let us rejoice!"

But my throat was hard with tears and the joy and marvel of it were gone when he fell to his knees. A torrent of tears soaked his scarred cheeks, flowing into his beard as he moaned,

"Damascus! At last! But brothers! It is such a long way from home!"

THE LOST TRIBE

Sydney 1959

When young, I was convinced that there was no alternative to being me, here. As imperative as this seemed, there was another knowledge, hazy, overlaid; a mere intimation, a little like a half-forgotten song, the lyrics lingering beyond the touch of the tongue. I could not hear all the melody. Only a few notes, sometimes. I knew they were part of a greater thing. I knew it with a vague certainty I could not doubt.

Sometimes in the quiet of early waking, or at dusk, when the bird song ceased and the Ibis flew in flocks to a nesting tree, this other knowledge would come, quietly. At the first intimation of its presence I usually turned my attention away to immediate, mundane concerns. My awareness of it disappeared like water into sand, so I wondered little about it. My life, like my youthful attention, became swamped by concerns as commonplace as they are universal. Awareness of anything other became soaked up by desires, needs and wants, as it does all those who grow up schooled in the early exercise of acquisition. Voices I did not recognize told me what to seek and what to strive to achieve. I soon learned how best to do what I was told.

At eighteen I was a clumsy youth. Because of my long thin limbs, diffident look and tentative movements, I was what used to be called 'gangling'. Consumed by an agonizing self-consciousness, my attention was so taken up by insecurity that the other knowledge, though known to be there, could not dawn.

Wonder of wonders! Though stumbling through life like a youth blindfolded, hobbled and let loose in a minefield, I met, wooed and won Josephine McCloud. Dear Jo. Why this delectable creature should have been vulnerable to my bungling attentions is inexplicable. Looking back, I marvel all the more. Was it because she felt secure in the knowledge of having an unattractive lover other women would not challenge her for?

Ashleigh once affirmed, with his characteristic contempt, and with an arrogant shake of his head to get his forelock out of his eyes – "The alliances we forge are inspired by complementary or opposing weaknesses of character" – causing a hiatus by groping in the pocket of his safari jacket for a box of matches, selecting one with slow deliberation to light his pipe.

Ashleigh was the leader, the chief, elected by a wordless consensus in deference to his personality, vitality and intelligence - perhaps accomplished by some ancient process of tribal law. Other equally hidden dynamics lay behind the intense energies that played within and between us all, linking us in an unseen, mostly unknown web. The conservative ones stayed within the group most of the time, others circled about it as moons do planets. Some, comet-like flashed through one group after another; free spirits heading for distant galaxies. We knew of other groups linked by different interests and leaders but gave them little attention. And so the dance was danced. The greatest unspoken and unrecognized need was to belong. I can see it now, for time, like space, lends perspective. Yet for me, the need was never met. The other knowledge, equally unspoken and so barely recognized, kept me always other. Did they know I was not really one of them, I wonder? – Yes, I think they did.

The war came. After agonies of indecision I decided to be a fighter pilot. That way I could be aloft and alone at least some of the time. So I joined the air force though I was fearful of billets, eating en masse, the horror of enforced company. Disqualified by color blindness and other disabilities I was forced to endure a desk job. I spent spirit-numbing years in the company of officious officers, bored clerks and assorted riff-raff. Efficient at everything, it was Ashleigh who became the pilot. I envied him. Even when I heard he had been killed on his first sortie out of Moresby.

In those years the other knowledge often hummed loudly in my ears. Though the changes were great, there was no change in the old tribal laws amongst those I lived and worked with at HQ. The clubs formed as naturally as birds flock together.

Fearful of my aloneness, I ingratiated myself as best I might with as many as I could. Oh! How I tried! My ghost went gambling, drinking and whoring, took up smoking, cursing, often staying up late drinking cheap booze, swapping lies and telling dirty jokes. A measure of my success, though one tinged with a hint of disapproval, was the nickname they gave me – 'The Flitter'. Sometimes, while almost believing that I belonged, the other would come. Just as a boy becoming aware of being observed in some misdemeanor slinks off, I would 'do a flit'. It seemed then, that I was a character in someone else's dream, but had woken up.

In the final year of boredom I sunk into depression, lassitude, nausea and jaundice and was delighted when the MO diagnosed Hepatitis, consigning me to a small infirmary with a window overlooking a park. Close by there was a huge old tree with a magpies nest high in its branches. I malingered there as long as I could. There was a collusion of sorts with the MO who let me get away with it because he didn't give a damn anyway. And he needed a partner at chess and someone to talk to about the English poets and the works of D.H. Lawrence. By the time the pretence of my malingering could no longer be credibly supported, the bombs had been dropped on Japan and the war was over.

The madness of being human produces a sort of relief when war is declared and euphoria when peace breaks out. We danced and sang, squandered food coupons, and ate jealously stored rarities. Others sat in lonely places, wondering. Some for the first time wept their sorrows away.

New tribes from a dozen different countries came to Australia. Tribal conflicts were common, but what could this mean to me, who belonged to none? It was easy to be successful in the new world that grew out of the old carcass. I look back with wry humor on a successful career as a salesman, realizing that it was made easy by a national passion to buy something. Though I wanted for nothing, and lived a comfortable life, it was haunted by a dark shadow cast by something dense and huge. Something ancient and indifferent, that I could not, dared not, fathom.

Like an actor playing a part and mouthing someone else's script I asked Jo to marry me. Playing her part, she said yes. Poor dear Jo. Strange and faithful, she became a housewife, resident on a dreary housing estate where rows of little fibro houses lined the streets in a soulless outer suburb. She became a mother in the second and fourth year of our marriage with an unquestioning, fatalistic resignation. It was almost palpable. I could feel the breeze of it waft about her when we passed in the hall and the little surges of it puffing out of her during the ritual acts of sex on Saturday nights.

Years of somnambulistic respectability passed, lived as in an ill-lit tunnel. Now that they are a memory it seems like a film I saw of someone else's life as I sat watching in the dark. Not long after our youngest child left home to be close to the university, Jo left me to live with a salesman she met when he was selling vacuum cleaners from door to door. The film I was watching was finished. The lights came on. My life was my own again. Eventually Jo leaving me was as welcome as the Hepatitis had been. I felt the gentle stirrings of some prodigious thing so much that I invited the other and was not fearful of it when it nuzzled at the edges of my awareness.

I thought: I have lived all my life as loudly as I could so not to hear the subversive messages it was darkly whispering. Does it matter now if I stopped? It was not an easy thing to do. Little by little I gave in to it, learning to trust it in little things. As I did so I cared less for all the things I held dear, thought were right and important. Soon, I was not a member of the club. Any club. Any group. I began to know the joy and freedom of being wholly my own. A joy made more exquisite for the sadness it brought. Radical changes came as naturally as seasons. I found myself sleeping happily on saggy old mattresses in small rooms in run down pubs in slum suburbs of the city, by days wandering the city looking with new, clear eyes.

I met one of my kind as we were both lounging about an inner city park. Archibald Ebeneza introduced himself, explaining that the name might not last the week, so if I met him again, I was not to assume that it would still be his name. This he said with a wry smile and a humorous twinkle in his one good eye. This seemed reasonable enough to me so I said I understood and that my name was anything he felt inclined to call me. He laughed happily, wiping his beard with a grubby hand.

"Hmm," he mused, "You look like a Bertram to me. For today anyhow. Mind if I call you Bert for short? Still a bit cold of nights, so I hole up in that pipe there. One Saturday Morning Herald is all a bloke needs to keep warm."

The other said this was the thing to do too, so I asked him did he mind if I shared it with him – for a while, anyway.

"Only till one of us leaves," he said.

Exhilarated with the joy of it, I waved goodbye and wandered on.

That night I returned to the old storm water pipe in the park by the bay. Archibald Ebeneza had a little fire going. He wasn't alone. Other vagrants leaned against the plastic bags that contained their belongings, listening sombrely to Bea Miles reciting Shakespeare sonnets.

"This is my friend Bert," Archibald said.

Gday: How's things? Come in: Take a load off yer feet: Squat here, they said. Bea Miles shouted for quiet. I felt quite at home.

...There is a slow, secret life hidden in the seething city. We are hundreds, bonded by intransigence, poverty and freedom. We are bonded by our pride in being scorned, patronized or ignored by those who can never know how much we pity them. They know I am one of them – the society of vagabonds. We belong to none but ourselves. It had taken a long time for me to find my way back home.

OUR VALLEY

Bellingen NSW 1996

Well, if I am going to tell you about our valley, maybe I should explain the lay of the land. But not so you could find this place and come to live here. There have been enough new settlers around here. It started in the late sixties. I came here in the early seventies, so I've been here in the valley thirty odd years now. I'm almost a local.

'Course, the real locals are the families who go back to the early days, descendants of those mad bastards dressed in calico and worsted who chopped their way here through the timber or came up the coast walking the beaches and swimming the rivers, to gnaw at the primeval forests till there was none left. Later they sailed up the rivers and built towns and the ships took the plundered forests away to build houses in the growing cities around the world. Then the same lot took to farming after the good timber had gone, growing corn and sugar cane. Then, when everyone ate lots of butter and mothers cooked scones and cakes most days, to dairy farming and butter making. Now they fatten cattle mostly and sell off bits of their holdings when they can to people who get to be new settlers and their sons and daughters go to university and live in cities and come home in flash cars sometimes, for holidays.

This valley is 'up north' to most cities in Australia; as the crow flies, about thirty kilometers from the coast I reckon. Maybe a bit more. Anyhow, there is a river called the Never-Never that flows out of the ravines of the great divide where the valley runs into the foothills. It's as clear as sunlight and fast flowing and you can feel the dark and chill of the mountain gorges in it. In the deep pools you can see boulders and stones shot from ancient volcanoes laying quiet and still now, and you see them like they were just under a pane of glass

Well, that Never-Never runs just past my place where the casaurinas grow in the gravel near the big bend; by the ruins of the old butter factory where the big tallowwood fell last flood. It goes right down the valley, following the mountains for a while. Then the big river mooches off to the coast right from one end of the valley to the other and on each side those green hills go rollicking about. These last few years pretty slick houses got built on some of those hills and it gives me the shits to see them perched up there. Business people from the big town up the coast mostly I expect. But along the river the locals still farm. There are cows and horses in the paddocks along with the old houses with the big verandahs and often a huge old fig tree been there a couple of hundred years and still going strong.

Then you come out onto the highway but that word highway is a bit of a joke; anyway, there it goes, up north, down south, pretty busy most of the time.

From there it's real flat till the river gets to the ocean where it gets a bit confused and goes this way and that and gets into mangrove channels and filters out into the Pacific. There is a little town there with a few shops and a café. It's got big figs in the street and camphor laurels big as water tanks and the branches covered in moss and lichens and a sort of orchid, big staghorns and birds nest ferns. They're sort of special, being right there in the street. If you get the corner seat in the café by the window you can look right up into them and see an old Mopoke sleeping sometimes as you enjoy a slab of Mavis' carrot cake.

It beats thinking about to wonder how long – like millions of years maybe - this valley of ours grew here all on its own with hardly a black going into it even, before we lot got here. Sometimes I go up to the top of Preston's hill, the last cleared one before the range and look down the valley towards the coast. There's bits of thirty or fifty year regrowth mostly on the ridges and the tops but as far as I can see in every direction except up the escarpment was forest so dense and the trees so big and high that the blokes that tried to follow the river up on foot took a day to go a mile. Not one tree of the original forest left. Bloody incredible. It's only one hundred and fifty years, about. Still it happened, and here we are.

And what about those first families that drove their cattle up the beaches to get here when there wasn't another human being in a week's riding and everything was strange and new and a lot of it was dangerous too. And tight about them was this dense forest hiding secrets in its darkness and they were right in the middle of it all alone. Being human is nothing special as far as the wilderness is concerned because you're just another animal in it. It spooks me to think about it.

Out of town is a cemetery where the old settlement used to be, not far from the old wharf where the sailing ships tied up. I go there sometimes to read the gravestones. It looks as though if you got to be older than five, say, you got a good chance to get older still. It looks like most families lost half their babies first year or so. Reading the grave stones, there were a lot of early deaths; falls from horses, drownings, accidents in mills or forest. Here are a few I wrote down:

"Bert Brown. Drowned crossing the bar. 2nd March 1868 Age 26"

"Robert Augue. Accidentally killed at Lady Belle mine Nana creek 5th January 1864. Aged 26". This one had me wondering how many had been killed at the mine by intention. A bush bard had written this for him –

> *"Remorseless death amongst us comes, and bitter grief imparts,*

And takes the loved ones from our homes but never
from our hearts."
"John McGuire, killed driving a team down the moun-
tain. 1869. Erected by his mates."

If you got to be five and had ambitions to get to be twenty it was smart not to ride horses. There are shootings and a few spearings too. But for the original settlers there are no gravestones. Those killed by the forest go unrecorded.

The first blokes came here about 1840. It wasn't all that long ago, and here we are by some incredible chance living here with pumps and tractors and running water and electric light, and stoves all you have to do is put a match to. Those first blokes were very different from us and so was every thing else. A lot of the hippies hereabouts reckon that the aborigines (Koories they call them) never came up the valley on account of it was too powerful, had heavy vibes. They reckon this valley has 'too much energy, man'. Come to think of it, there is a difference from the coast you can't help noticing. Along the coast it's mostly flat and there's a lot of scrub and not many big trees. And it's cooler in summer and warmer in winter, except when the southerlies blow up the coast. But as you come up the road from the highway things change. There are hills about with tight little gullies with thirty to fifty year regrowth. Then when you get to the range where the big trees and vines grow up the steeps it really is different. In the summer it rains a lot – the edge of the monsoons they get further up north. The forest gets hot and steamy and the quiet still air smells rich with humus and moulds. Down on the river flats the air smells of the river and breezes blow from way out to sea and the hills are bright green all year round.

People silly enough to have a lawn can see the grass grow while they're putting the mower back in the shed. Your clothes go mouldy and stink and you can't see your shoes for blue fungus. In the winter there is little rain and the sun is gentle and a good day is better than good days anywhere in the world. It's cool enough to do hard work with just a little sweat and the sky's a clear blue with not one cloud from sunup to sundown. In the evening, out walking as the sun sets you can feel wafts of warm air around your bare legs like the brushings of a friendly cat and the old Mopokes fly out of the forest and sit on the fence posts keeping an eye out for some tucker.

Energy? Well I reckon you could say so. The blokes with lawns and mowers know about it. The way things grow here you wouldn't believe, but it's not just that fact but it is the electricity. Even on a clear night with no storm about, the sky flickers with light. It's a thing to see in the winter sometimes when there's no moon and it's very dark, the lightning flashing away in the distance in all directions. So maybe they are right about the abos but I reckon that if they didn't come up the valley the bloody leaches might have had a lot to do with it.

Sometimes when I'm having a beer with Bert or Charley I say "Here's to the past – at least you can rely on that!" Or sometimes I say, "Here's to the past – it's the only thing you can rely on!" They just smile but there's plenty of past in the pub. The Empire pub is a relic. (So's the Empire, come to that.) The only good thing about the pub apart from the beer are the photos around the walls. There are faded old prints of droghers paddling timber down the river, trading vessels sailing over the bar, and Cobb and Co. coaches outside the pub about the turn of the century. There's one of a boat picnic with the boat crammed with over-dressed people and all the blokes with straw boaters on their heads and not one male or woman without a big hat. And a milk dray heavy with milk cans stuck in the mud and scruffy kids wearing long shorts and braces looking on. A coach-and-four lying broken at the bottom of a gully – that sort of thing.

I once knew a sociologist who said that you could learn a lot about a town by its pubs. Met him in the back bar of the old Empire actually. Couldn't have thought much of us. This was when I first came up here and the pub was as grotty as only a pub can be.

Stunk of stale beer and old butts and vomit out the back. A lane leads from the road along one side of the pub to a vacant block behind where cars park. The lane is still called the 'carriageway'. It's dry and dusty and rutted and you step onto the pub verandahh on old sleepers taken from the railway. On the verandahh is a few old tables and chairs. Other side of the carriageway is the old Emporium that once sold everything you would find in a whole town of shops. It was as run down as the pub.

Back then, the town was dying because the dairy industry was having a bad time. There were empty shops with old papers scrunched in the doorways blowing about with leaves and dust. Some of the shops hadn't had a coat of paint since Adam was a boy. All but a bit of the grand old Emporium was bare and idle. The pub was rickety and needed a coat of paint and the white ants had had a good go at it. The stairway to the first floor was shaky and it wasn't smart to lean against the rails of the verandah where the blokes liked to drink on Saturday afternoon with the races blaring from the big 'His Master's voice' radio that stood four feet high at the top of the stairs. The way the old pub looked it was hard to tell it from a council dunny. Lots of tiles everywhere and in the dunny that chemical smell from blocks of some sort of disinfectant in the urinals.

Now here's a thing – the way things blokes wrote on dunny walls has changed so much. They tell me that the woman's dunnies are where the real crude stuff is. I don't know if that's true though the old community hall had a dunny that was what would be called unisex these days and there was pretty ribald stuff in that one. Heavy ones too about women's lib and anti-male ones. One was ' women need men like fish need bicycles'. I got a pen and scribbled 'so how did you get here then?' underneath it. There were some humdingers on those walls. There was 'subvert the dominant paradigm' so I had to ask my mates what the hell it meant and it was a while before I found out. I liked 'sex is better than logic but I can't prove it' and the silly ones like 'Mickey

Mouse is a Jew'. Anyhow in 1978 they pulled the community hall down which caused a great deal of fuss and I've forgotten the best ones.

There's been a lot of changes since I came here when you stop to think of it. They creep up on a man one by one so you don't notice it till it's all happened. That reminds me of one of those things someone wrote in the dunny – one of those clever ones – it said 'Permanent change is here to stay.' When a person gets to my age you can have a gut full of it. I reckon the planet too is reeling from it. Too much has changed too fast. Some of us are addicted to it along with all them other things. Hooked. Change for the sake of it. Doesn't matter where it leads. Irresponsible change gets called progress and we follow that banner no matter where it leads.

Not much pleases me the way things are now. I suppose that's the reason I'm in this little house alone in the bush and don't have much to do with anybody. I'd rather it was a hundred years ago. Don't get me wrong; I'm not one of those Luddites. Like everyone, I'm grateful for all those things that make life easier. I just don't think they make it better. I reckon the price is too high. I bet Mother Nature thinks so. The price the poor old world has paid is death and starvation and all sorts of ugliness put by us on what used to be meadow and forest and streams and so much of the living ground stifled under cement and asphalt it's hard for the poor old earth to breathe.

Now I can't argue that the old ute isn't real handy but my life would be a lot simpler without it, and boy, would I save some money! That old ute is my major cost in life. And when it goes bung it's a pain in the arse. Now a horse would cost me next to nothing and its emissions would be environmentally friendly and useful on the veggies. I reckon it must have been a great life here-abouts a hundred years ago. They didn't need to know half the things we have to to get by and a bloke could do most everything for himself. No need for electricians, mechanics, plumbers, accountants, builders, you name it. Now a bloke needs a battalion of other blokes to keep his show running.

I think a lot about how it must have been. Struth! Imagine coming out from little old green England six months in a sailing boat to a place like this in the old days! I know what you're thinking. Silly old bugger living in the past. There aren't many present-time people anyhow as far as I can see. Most of us are future-time people. We hurry through the present like a thief being chased by a policeman. It's only when the present moment is so good that we can't ignore it any longer that we pay it any attention. Then right off we are off into the future planning how to make it happen again.

It's true though, I do think about the past a lot. But that doesn't mean I'm living in it all the time. It's a funny business. When I think about my own past it is clearer than when it happened because when it happened I was too busy being somewhere else. When I think about life in the total, like looking down the valley from the escarpment it seems to be like Shakespeare said. 'A tale told by an idiot'. But a tale nonetheless. That's the important bit. Youngens don't know because they can't see the rest of their life. They're flat out dreaming the future. I'm not even sure if babies are present-time people. Maybe they are for a bit, but not for long. Soon as they start thinking about when the next feed is coming or learn about Christmas the present gets to be merely a doorway.

We've all got time on our hands. It's like a bottomless pit and we try to fill it up with all sorts of things but it just swallows it all up. Rich people think time is money. Most of us think time is progress. Ambitious people reckon that every hour should be sixty minutes of achievement. I read somewhere that 'time is nature's way of preventing everything from happening at once' which doesn't make the slightest bit of sense to me because whatever happens is always at once. My dad had a funny saying about real tall blokes. He'd say 'Cripes! He's as long as a wet weekend!' All in all, I reckon time of any sort is a bit of a bummer and I'm glad it's running out. You go on day after day running your life-support systems but it's mostly just a habit when you're old. And even if life's crook it's such a habit you don't want to give it up.

Time's as weird as eternity. Seems to me sometimes, both are only notions. Sometimes nothing looks as though it is real when I get to thinking about things. I mean, duration is a fact but this time thing isn't. I wonder if the abos had time? Anyhow, whatever, it's a mystery to me. Look, the present is as slippery as quicksilver isn't it? As far as I'm concerned the future is a figment, the present doesn't exist until it is over, so the past is really all we got. No use running away from the fact. There's nothing worse than being locked into the present. It's like wearing blinkers. There's all the past and all the future like an infinite highway and here we are on this little speck of a present and it seems to fill the lot. God! I think up some pretty strange notions when I sit on the verandah on my old well-cushioned wicker chair and look down the valley. Sometimes I sit and just look. I reckon that bump of tree tops on the horizon is about where the river rounds the bend near the town. Other times I get a sudden flash and stop thinking to look at it. It's like seeing the wraith of a ghost disappearing around a corner. Days later there it is clear and sharp. Then comes others I know were the first flash turning up from another angle. This keeps up till it's all done and I can get to know how it all fits together. That's how I get to know things I've never been taught.

Sometimes I think this might have something to do with the job I did for so many years. I used to be a Linotype operator in the old hot metal days before the new technology put the type-setting machines out of business. There I sat at the keyboard in front of this big mechanical monster and words poured through my eyes and out my fingers a slug at a time. When I worked at the Sydney Morning Herald three floors up in the fine old building on the corner of Pitt and Hunter streets, there used to be twenty of us all in a row and we set up quite a clatter I can tell you. For a long time I worked for a firm of printers and clattered my way through books about all sorts of things. You don't stop to ponder about what you're setting. Maybe I have soaked up things without knowing about it, and those ghosts of notions that pop into my old head have something to do with all those words I've typed and maybe one of those books was about time.

My son gave me a pocket computer. Buggered if I know why because I've got nothing to compute. Wondering about being alive, I got it out and figured out how many days I had lived. It comes to about 25 000 days not counting being a baby and a kid. I don't count them because I can't remember them, but if I did count them it would be 29 200. It seems to me that when you look back it's a history isn't it? – And history is mostly fiction. When you look back you can't remember everything or know about all the circumstances. You just know your little bit and that's all mixed up anyhow. So I reckon we are a figment of our own imagination and what we think is our past isn't as true as we like to believe.

Sometimes when I'm having a beer with Bert or Charley I say "Here's to the past – at least you can rely on that!" Or sometimes I say 'Here's to the past – it's the only thing you can rely on!" They just smile but there's plenty of past in the pub. The Empire pub is a relic. (So's the Empire, come to that.) The only good thing about the pub apart from the beer are the photos around the walls. There are faded old prints of droghers paddling timber down the river, trading vessels sailing over the bar, and Cobb and Co. coaches outside the pub about the turn of the century. There's one of a boat picnic with the boat crammed with overdressed people and all the blokes with straw boaters on their heads and not one male or female without a big hat. And a milk dray heavy with milk cans stuck in the mud and scruffy kids wearing long shorts and braces looking on. A coach-and-four lying broken at the bottom of a gully – that sort of thing.

I once knew a sociologist who said that you could learn a lot about a town by its pubs. Met him is the back bar of the old Empire actually. Couldn't have thought much of us. This was when I first came up here and the pub was as grotty as only a pub can be. Stunk of stale beer and old butts and vomit out the back. A lane leads from the road along one side of the pub to a vacant block behind where cars park. The lane is still called the 'carriageway'. It's dry and dusty and rutted and you step onto the pub verandah on old sleepers taken from the railway. On the verandah is a few old tables and chairs. Other side of the carriageway is the old Emporium that once sold everything you would find in a whole town of shops. It was as run down as the pub.

Back then, the town was dying because the dairy industry was having a bad time. There were empty shops with old papers scrunched in the doorways blowing about with leaves and dust. Some of the shops hadn't had a coat of paint since Adam was a boy. All but a bit of the grand old Emporium was bare and idle. The pub was rickety and needed a coat of paint and the white ants had had a good go at it. The stairway to the first floor was shaky and it wasn't smart to lean against the rails of the verandah where the blokes liked to drink on Saturday afternoon with the races blaring from the big 'His Master's voice' radio that stood four feet high at the top of the stairs. The way the old pub looked it was hard to tell it from a council dunny. Lots of tiles everywhere and in the dunny that chemical smell from blocks of some sort of disinfectant in the urinals.

Now here's a thing – the way things blokes wrote on dunny walls has changed so much. They tell me that the woman's dunnies are where the real crude stuff is. I don't know if that's true though the old community hall had a dunny that was what would be called unisex these days and there was pretty ribald stuff in that one. Heavy ones too about women's lib and anti-male ones. One was ' women need men like fish need bicycles'. I got a pen and scribbled 'so how did you get here then?' underneath it.

There were some humdingers on those walls. There was 'subvert the dominant paradigm' so I had to ask my mates what the hell it meant and it was a while before I found out. I liked 'sex is better than logic but I can't prove it' and the silly ones like 'Mickey Mouse is a Jew'. Anyhow in 1978 they pulled the community hall down which caused a great deal of fuss and I've forgotten the best ones.

There's been a lot of changes since I came here when you stop to think of it. They creep up on a man one by one so you don't notice it till it's all happened. That reminds me of one of those things someone wrote in the dunny – one of those clever ones – it said 'Permanent change is here to stay.' When a person gets to my age you can have a gut full of it. I reckon the planet too is reeling from it. Too much has changed too fast. Some of us are addicted to it along with all them other things. Hooked. Change for the sake of it. Doesn't matter where it leads. Irresponsible change gets called progress and we follow that banner no matter where it leads.

Not much pleases me the way things are now. I suppose that's the reason I'm in this little house alone in the bush and don't have much to do with anybody. I'd rather it was a hundred years ago. Don't get me wrong; I'm not one of those Luddites. Like everyone, I'm grateful for all those things that make life easier. I just don't think they make it better. I reckon mostly, the price is too high. I bet Mother Nature thinks so. The price the poor old world has paid is death and starvation and all sorts of ugliness put by us on what used to be meadow and forest and streams and so much of the living ground stifled under cement and asphalt it's hard for the poor old earth to breathe.

Now take Frank Worral for instance. Frank went to the city when he left school. He came back looking like something from the flower pavilion at the Show. There wasn't one part of him that wasn't a different colour. He had tattoos on his toes. You could see them sticking out of his sandals when he didn't have his purple socks on, and his pants were patched with bits of coloured material all over. His shirts were what they call psychedelic and he wore vests sometimes, like the oldies used to but his were covered with buttons about things like whales or protesting about something with words like 'If you are not part of the solution, you're part of the problem!' But it seems to me that if you are part of the solution you *are* the problem. To top it all his hair was as long as a woman's and curled and you couldn't see his face for beard. He wore bright berets with big pompoms on them too. Not to mention the few with scarlet hair standing up in spikes. They would have wondered at the hugging maybe. Hugging is in. I've even seen oldies doing a big hug right in the main street. The hippie types hug so long you think maybe you are looking at Siamese twins.

The other day I read somewhere that the blacks have been in Australia for 40 000 years, minimum. Christ! Just think of it! All that time and hardly any change. Until we lot came, not enough to bother thinking about anyhow. I got my computer and worked it out. That's 14 600.000 days. All that time and the blacks hardly left a mark on the landscape. Or an impact on the ecology as they would say these days. Like sleeping years in a bed and not leaving a wrinkle on the sheets. We lot wouldn't think that was any good. We're hooked on change. The worst torture a judge could inflict on a crim instead of ten years in solitary would be a few days in one of those float tank things without anything happening at all.

God, how this valley has changed! I can only try to imagine what it must have been like before we stripped it and all the exotic trees and weeds and plants took over. It's like me falling in love with my ideal woman the same age as me – nudging eighty - and me feeling deprived because there was no way I could know her when she was young and fresh and beautiful. It's a bit bloody late but some people are beginning to look after the valley now. I was talking to a bloke the other day who was a bit down because of the drought affecting the native trees he had planted. 'Looks

like you'll have to get the watering can and water them that way'
I said. 'You've got to be kidding!' he said, 'All three thousand of
them?' Well there's one bloke who has put a few back.

This valley has been going through its slow changes for maybe millions of years and might be a lot smarter than we give it
credit for. It's taken Lantana and Camphor Laurel and Paspalum,
Kikuyu and a hundred others and made them one of its own. We
can't be sure it's not using us. Maybe in another few thousand
years we will be long gone and there will be a different sort of
wilderness and the valley will have used us all for compost.

How do you reckon it would be if a few of the first settlers
were brought back from the dead and plonked in the main street
of the town they pioneered way back in the 1840,s? We can't
know anything about how it was like to be alive in the pioneer-
ing days. Those old-timers were not living in the same world for
a start. I reckon it would scare them shitless like the blacks were
when they turned up. Or how we would be if a few extraterres-
trials turned up on their space ship down the oval when the big
footy match was on and everybody was in town. Imagine it! The
shock would be about the same for those old timers. It wouldn't
just be the cars and the huge timber trucks roaring down the
road but the people too. At the sight of some of us the old timers would go looking for a shotgun or the women would take to
them with their umbrellas or go looking for a copper.

There were a lot of Scots amongst the early settlers; stiff, dour
Protestants. The valley had plenty of Methodists and Presbyte-
rians who had the sort of stuff to be pioneers. Believing you had
the right and only God and that the earth was yours to do what
you liked with was a big help. Now there are plenty of people
they wouldn't want to know and they would go get their shot-
guns or call out the troopers.

The old ute broke down one day on the way out from town
and a bloke pulled up in a beat-up old Holden.

"Hari Om!" he says. "Can I help you?"

"G'day Harry," I says. "Me name's Ted. She's conked on me and I can't get her started".

"Let's have a look" He says and got out of the old Holden. He was dressed in a sort of loose orange outfit like a sheet around his waist and a billowing shirt without a collar and he had these big beads around his neck. He was a nice bloke though and got me going with a bit of know-how about carbies.

"You going to the Kirtain?" he says.

"Eh? What curtains?" I says, not catching on.

"Oh curtains!" He says laughing. "No not curtains, Kirtain. We sing and play drums and organs and dance too. Then we have a feast"

"Well good for you!" I says, "Sounds like a good time is had by all eh? How about John Denver – do you sing any of his songs? I like his songs a lot."

"Not in a Kirtain, no. In a Kirtain you only sing the names of God".

Well, this bit of information had me a bit foxed. I thought maybe he was pulling my leg.

"Oh" I says, "How many names has God got then?"

"Thousands! Millions! Countless actually." He looked at me as if he was about to tell me the most important bit of information, then he looked around the forest and up to the sky.

"Everything's a name of God," he says. "Struth alive! as my old dad would say. This earnest young man might be a bit of a nut but he had a face as round and smooth as a baby's bum and I like him nevertheless.

"Well no," I told him. "I live up by the range and was going home when she conked".

"The Ashram's up the valley. Why don't you come too? Everybody is invited and the food's really Satvic!" he says, licking his chops.

Well, I didn't have an inkling of what he was talking about but I thought, 'why not - Music and free tucker, what's the harm?'

So I followed him out through the forest but when he got to the fork he turned down a dirt track and followed the river for a bit where there is a big old homestead put up by one of the old-timers back in the 1890's. It was surrounded by shrubs and fruit trees all doing well. Inside was a big room lined with silky oak with doors leading out onto the verandah where everybody left their shoes. There must have been near thirty people in the room, not one over forty that made me feel sort of out of it but nobody seemed to mind. Except for two or three I suppose you would say most of them were hippies though that word is not as strong as it used to be. Some would just call them alternatives. Even the kids were sitting still as frogs, eyes closed, with their mums. Others played on the verandah. Everyone was sitting cross-legged on the floor, some on little cushions. It was quiet as the morgue until they started up banging the little metal disk things together and the hand organ and the drums started up in a sort of a dirge-like thing and then everybody started singing Harry's name out then lots of other words I didn't know. Talk about weird! It was so weird I was enjoying it better than the Show by a long shot.

One of the mums had a breast out with a newborn sucking. One of the kids rolled side to side on the floor picking its nose. Mum gave the hand a bit of a flick and says "Waterfall, stop that!" After a while the chanting got me in and I started too, along with everybody else. It wasn't too hard seeing that there were only a few words they sang and after a bit you couldn't help it. Things got real worked up and they left me behind. The drums and hand organ were going sixty to the dozen and some got up and did wavy dances on their own and the others rocked back and forward. Then they slowed right down to a whisper and stopped. The silence was so loud I could hear my guts squeezing the tucker through. They kept this up for nearly two hours. It got a bit rich for me so I went out onto the verandah like I had seen some others do. That's where the mums with restless kids were and I started in to play a bit with the youngens. One lad had the name of Thunder and another was Baroom and a girl was called Sky and another Bright Dawn. They were beaut kids but I felt sorry for them when they got to school. Life would be hell if the other kids were anything like the ratbags I went to school with.

When it was over, about six o'clock, big pots of tucker were brought out onto the table on the verandah and everybody tucked in. We all sat on a strip of carpet along the wall and most ate their food with their fingers of all things! I couldn't figure out why they did that. I didn't want to stick out like a sore thumb so I tried it too and made a bit of a mess of it. It was bloody good tucker though. They had a sort of a spiced pea soup that went real well with rice so I went back for seconds. Sitting there, it was a real education for me to hear the sort of talk that went on. A lot of it I couldn't understand because it was 'in' talk. I knew about that from other groups I had run in to. The lingo doesn't make much sense until you get the meaning of a few key words or sayings, then if you use your nous you can understand a bit or make a few remarks not too far off the mark. What got me was how much talk said nothing or was vague as hell. One earnest young bloke was talking to a young girl next to me but I couldn't make much sense of what he was on about. He said something like "...he went to his ajna chakra and saw that I had a lot of karma to work through about the glands, specially the thyroid and I just know he's right-on because I always get this spacey feeling there" And the girl just says, "Wow eh? Far out...Wow. Cool" But what that meant I don't know. Then she says, "Eating meat is so gross I can't handle it. The Guru says that if you eat meat and garlic you're done for. Your vibrations go down. You know, too heavy. Alcohol too. Makes you gross and it's heavy karma but a bit of grass is OK eh?" Then it was his turn. "Yeh. Good. Cool. It lifts the vibes. Definitely. Yeah," he says. There was talk about dolphins talking and organic gardening and natural childbirth and acupuncture and Elephant gods and Goddesses – enough to send a good Scots Presbyterian spluttering for a wee dram. So here they are, these far children of the originals taking up foreign religions from a subject race their grandfathers didn't have much time for. That's hard enough for some of the locals to swallow let alone the old timers who thought a Koolgardie Safe and a mangle were technological marvels and that the sun would never set on the Empire.

But it's funny how some of the Swamis in the Ashram have got to some of the oldies like me. Some of the farmers take them produce from time to time and stay for a chat and a cup of cha. Of course, they never go to the classes they hold but you can tell that they like the people and don't mind the Ashram being there.

When you get to my age you see more and more dead bodies. Your friends and family go, one by one. Sentimentality aside, it's like looking at a matchstick after it's blown out. You can tell where the flame used to be. You see where your friend used to burn, lying there. A husk. Like a cicada shell. I've never understood what all the hullabaloo about death is all about. For me it's just another fact of life and I'm grateful for it. We're so neurotic about it that we try to hide it away so when it pops into our life we get a rude shock and say, how awful! That's one of the big differences between us and the tough bastards that pioneered this place. They lived with it. Diphtheria, Mumps and Measles were killers as sure as Typhoid and Cholera and there were plenty of them too. If they had a fancy to fry a chop they had to go and slit a sheep's throat, draw and quarter it and slice off the bit they wanted to eat. Guts gore and dead bodies were one of the things a person lived with. Dead humans as well. Most everybody would have seen a couple before they grew up. I reckon that's what gave them that get-up-and-go, that lust for life that fired their boilers. Lots of death grounded them too. They knew there wasn't much difference between life and a lit match.

Funny thing is, there's never been many rabbits in this grass-green valley. Some hares though. I shot one a week ago. He got into my veggie patch. Shot him with the old Lithgow .22 I bought way back in 1948. I popped him in the pot with some of my on-ions and a dollop of mustard and a big spud from out of my spud pit and he was bloody good I can tell you. Then it came to me like one of those flashes I was telling you about. That's the difference! ...Between life and death, that is. When you're alive you eat your environment. When you're dead, it eats you. Fair enough.

No use denying that an Aussie country town can be a bit of a dreary place and not much to look at either, but our town is something special. In the early days there was a doctor who was keen on trees and he imported seed and planted trees all over the place and that's one of the things that makes this town differ-ent. Then there are the people who are different from the run of country folk. Now you wouldn't believe it but for some reason this little town has more famous people than your average town by a country mile. Since the eighties they crept in one after the other. We have writers galore and a goofy and very famous pia-nist, a few media personalities and lots of well-known artists too. Maybe this is why Entrepreneurs pick this location for cultural events. The town is getting too well known for my liking.

This place is a cultural smörgåsbord enough to upset the di-gestion of the average well-traveled dilettante. No need to go overseas or to a big city to taste the trends of this crazy age. It all happens right here. There are a few notice boards about town where you can find out what's going on. There are notices about garage sales, lost animals, geese etc for sale, personal observa-tions re the state of the nation, indignant affirmations like *'will the bastard who stole the brush cutter out of my shed put it back or I will dob you in'*. (Ah, there is a story there because the dobber must know who the dobbee is). Another with an even more in-triguing story reads: *REQUIRED Room in share house with 1 or 2 others. Co-operative facilitated agreement towards active Develop-ments of domestic management. Policy of integrity and respect, No expectations, Sole criteria. Message for Barry.* I wondered about this one for weeks and still can't figure it out. Can't make head nor tail of it. My favorite is: *WANTED. Someone to fix my toaster.* Under this message is scribbled, *'CHUCK IT OUT'*. There are notices for courses such as 'How to be happy though human', 'Tapping your inner power', 'How to contact your angel', Psychic this and that, rebirthing workshops, requests, statements, performances, ads. It's a busy little town.

How is it that certain sorts of people gather at one place? It just sort of happens by some sort of instinct and can colour a whole town or suburb like Haight-Ashbury in San Francisco where all the poofters hang out or like Paris is for artists or New York for writers. This place was a Mecca for hippies in the sixties and it looked as though hippiedom was here to stay. The health food shop was the most thriving business in the town in those days but now it is a wonder how Fred manages to pay the rent. Now the town is getting trendy. We have a French Patisserie and a modern Supermarket too. Then people started buying acreages from the subdivisions of the old properties so big houses began to sit on top of the rolling hills out from the river flats. Then developers chopped up the paddocks around the edge of town so there are rows of nasty brick bungalows where the grass, cows, horses and trees used to be, bugger it. There's no doubt about it though, the biggest change the old valley has seen since we arrived was the hippie invasion. There they were, those hard working down-to-earth farmers struggling to make ends meet like maybe they had never had to do before, and in came this other mob living in another world. A world as far removed from the locals world as the whites world was from the blacks, not much more than a century before.

You know, up till the first World War a bloke could get by pretty well without much money at all if you had a bit of land and a horse and cow or two and a few pigs and chooks and grew all his own veggies. But then you were taught to want more than a bit of tucker and a change of clothes. Everybody had to have a radio set and other gadgets so you paid for poles and had power brought to your house. Then you had to have a car or a tractor or both and the petrol to run it with and soon you had your nose to the grindstone to pay for it all. That was called progress and they all thought it was wonderful. There were boom years and most got all these things and money in the bank as well. Then came the hard times, thanks to progress and they sold bits of their land and invested their money in secondary industry or went into trucking or timber or some such. Then the hippies moved in and rented the old disused bails or lived in sheds or built themselves some sort of shelter out in the bush or put their money together and bought land and started communes. They built houses out of mud or lived in tepees and went in for agriculture in a big way. One dope plant out along a creek in the deep bush and you could live well for years. Before you knew it the town began looking up. The shopkeepers began to smile. They might call them dole-bludgers but that didn't stop them taking their money. The locals were in a fix. Getting a bit of business in the town again was a welcome change but from an altogether unwelcome source. Farmers were happy selling off their land but didn't think much of the hippies talking about saving the earth and planting trees everywhere they had sweated getting rid of them. They complained that the women dressed like tarts and breast-fed in public and the blokes looked like poofters with long hair and scruffy beards and they didn't wash enough. Their old vans and cars fit for the scrap heap were covered with posters demanding the locals save the whales, stop felling the forest, watering their cows in the river, or stop using pesticides. You didn't want to be hit with all that every time you went to town.

They sang protest songs in the park on market day and their dirty kids played in the street with no clothes on and they weren't even Christians. Some of the locals suspected even worse things. Satanic rites and sexual orgies and that sort of thing. The letters to the editor column in the paper ran hot with complaint. So some of the hippies, stoned as usual, nailed a dead chook to the door of the manse and went behind the dunny in the park and giggled fit to burst. I bet they regretted that later. The local rag was full of it. It even made the Sydney papers. Sermons were preached about it for months. The ministers and congregations were grateful for the change and kept it going as long as they could. For years it was a standoff. If you wore a beard or an Indian cotton dress; if you sang songs and played a guitar; drove a VW wagon; wore beads or colourful pants you were a hippie. That meant you smoked dope, bludged on the dole, slept with anyone or maybe any two, didn't wash and were a threat to civilization as we know it. If you were a local of whatever caste you were a redneck. That meant you had no soul; a meat-eater out to destroy the planet by overgrazing, a careless user of fossil fuels, a person who wore blinkers and was anti intelligent change. You were a violent, greedy, thoughtless person who would rape and belt up the aborigines if there were any left. You supported the White Australia policy, voted for the Nationals and probably belonged to the RSL.

Well, that'll give you an idea of what the hippies and rednecks thought of each other back in the sixties. As for me, I went my own way. Sometimes I got blasted by both sides, like what happened when I was silly enough to run for council back in '78.

The hippie invasion really shook the valley up, like when the first whites arrived about 1840. People sold up and left after living here a life time. It came to outright war a few times, like when the council tried to pull down the old community hall where the hippies hung out. It's taken nearly twenty years to simmer down. It's still there of course,, but even the public disputes and tension is OK. There hasn't been a punch-up in years. There is a billiard table in the back bar of the pub where a lot of the clashes used to happen. On the wall is a blackboard for chalking up the score. Mid-eighties scores that ran down two columns were sometimes headed Hippies and Rednecks. There's been a lot of change on both sides.

Some of the farmers have been busted for growing dope, some of them have beards and play guitar and even swim in the river nude and their wives have gone mystical with imported religions. A lot of the old hippies have moved on to God knows where – office jobs in the city maybe. Some have gone into business and wear shoes. The ones on the communes live a lot like the old-timers, growing their own tucker and living simple without much money in their pockets. One of the most active ones in the seventies – Cliff Connors - was a real banner waver and led all sorts of protests. He started one of the first multiple occupancies and built his barn-like loft house way out in the Promised Land, without council approval of course, out of scraps of filched timber and stuff scrounged from demolition sites. After a series of hippie girl friends he up and married the daughter of the Church of England minister. He shaved his beard and cut his hair and took to trendy clothes. He moved into a brick bungalow in town with a neat lawn, had two kids and a big four-wheel drive and got into real estate. So he joined the Chamber of Commerce of course, then the Bowling club and started having a few beers with the shopkeepers down the RSL on Friday nights. I knew him real well and always thought he would call this valley home forever. But what do you reckon? He sold up and moved to Sydney and bought a place in the inner city and went into property development. Well that bamboozled me I can tell you. Funny old world, ay?

WHERE THE HEART IS

Plymouth 1836

It was a winter's day, the air dark and heavy with fog. The usual bustle of the docks was muffled, the cobbles and the timbers of the wharf gleamed dully with cold sleet. Wet rigging dropped beads of water onto the decks, the heads and backs of seamen getting the barque ready for sea.

In another part of Plymouth, a lad of about eighteen, soft whiskered and clumsy, stood waiting dazed with dread and excitement in the offices of McBride, Victor and Company, a firm of ship owners. He wore an old duffel coat, the toggles broken, the nap well worn down the back; perhaps it once belonged to a coachman. Under that, a doublet, soiled knee breeches and hose, on his large feet old give-away shoes cracked and without buckles.

"Well young fella-me-lad can 'e write?" said a clerk bringing a large heavily bound book to the counter.

"I can sign me name well enough" the boy said defensively, taking the quill. With slow deliberation he wrote in the column indicated by the ink stained finger, Hayward Redpath The finger moved to another column. "Now the date," said the clerk. The young man put his tongue between his lips, wrinkled his brows and wrote 20/2/1836. He was proud of his guile. He could not have written the date out in letters. At the top of the page were the words Passengers on the Stafford, bound for Port Jackson, New South Wales.

"Best look lively now m'lad. Report to Chief Officer Roberts aboard the Stafford. Ask where she be of the Dock Guard. Be off now, she's out on the tide."

The lad picked up his small cloth bag, obediently tugging his forelock and hurried out the door into the busy street. He looked about for a time as though stunned. 'I haven't even had time to see the city' he thought. 'Port Jackson won't be like this. Will there be streets and buildings even? – In a ship on the ocean! Half way 'round the world I'm going. Is this really me? Who would have thought such a thing!' Bumped by a passer-by he awoke to his present and started to walk briskly towards the docks.

His purposeful walk dwindled to a halt. A fear of not being came to him, the dark death of familiar things forsaken; of dimly sensed unknowns and the daunting apprehensions of unknown challenges he would surely have to face. He hid himself in a drainway between two buildings hoping to escape his fears. Hot tears came to his eyes as he shrank down in his duffel coat against the grimy wall. Behind the dread of the unknown loomed the memory of the life he knew. All he strove to be free from floated clear and wordless on the blackness before his closed eyes. He saw the stifling, unremitting squalor of the workhouse, smelt the stench, felt the everlasting hunger, worse those freezing winter nights too cold for the consolation of sleep. He felt the bruises, some given for his supposed benefit by the warders, some much harder to bear, from the bigger boys in exchange for his food. But then he saw too, the Governor that marvelous day he read the advertisement from the London Times, the day hope and purpose came into his life for the first time.

He heard the words...those British citizens, deemed worthy, of sound health and good character should apply in the first instance to the Secretary of State for the Colonies. The feeling of hope and purpose began to warm his soul again. He had to have a new future. He knew he had no choice.

The cloud lifted, his mind lightened. He hurried on. As he strode towards the docks he repeated to himself the words of Thomas Mitchell, the Surveyor General of that distant land; words that always filled him with wonder and awe.

"Land that for natural fertility and beauty could scarcely be surpassed...streams of unfailing abundance and plains covered with the richest pasturage. Stately trees and majestic mountains adorn the ever varying scenery."

The other truth was not told but that would not have deterred him now. It was four o'clock and almost dark when he found the Stafford. The strangeness of the ship awed him. Apprehensions darkened his mind again as the cabin boy took him below. The last companionway led down to an emigrants hold where rows of rickety bunks were lined one above the other along the hull and down the center of the hold. Dim oil lamps hung from the roof. When his eyes became adjusted to the poor light he could see figures crouched on the deck or dozing in the bunks. At the far end in the dim light a circle of men were playing cards. Strange odours hung in the stale air. Fearfully unsure, Hayward crept into a bunk, put his bag under his head and full of apprehension, found a little solace in a restless sleep.

Before dawn he lay awake, too apprehensive to get up. He listened with interest to the new sounds that filtered down from the decks above. The muffled cries of orders, the creak of timbers moving, the rattle of blocks and the lapping of water against the hull; the sounds of a ship making out to sea; about him other sounds familiar to him from the workhouse; stirrings, broken snores, sighs, whisperings, the sound of sullage buckets being used, stumbling and cursing.

When a seaman came into the hold carrying a lantern and shouted that they should file into the galley for victuals he laid waiting until last. Then he climbed down from his bunk and followed them to the galley for a breakfast of gruel, black coffee and an apple. They ate at a long table, mostly in silence. Unhappy memories tinged his thoughts so he kept his head down and spoke to nobody.

The Master came below decks and called them to attention.

"Well me hopefuls," he shouted holding his lantern high, "Tis possible ye may relish the next six months or so no better than the last, wherever ye came from. Land in the colonies is being sold at five shillin's an acre to pay for your passage and there's nary enough for our masters out o' that. Any seaman is an officer to yer so do as yer told by any of 'em for fear o' me. Keep out of the seaman's way and the focsle an women's hold is out o bounds, y' hear? Empty your sullage bucket when ye go up. An' you're to see this hold doesn't run in swill, so keep it swabbed. The ship's doctor will be about Mondays and Fridays. Pick yourselves a spokesman to air problems an' bring any grievances to me. I don't want every Tom, Dick an' Harry a- pesterin' the life out o' me. An' no hanky-panky with the women, mind. Sundays at the bell all passengers will gather aft at the quarterdeck for a reading of the Holy Book, weather permitting".

Hayward felt comfortable with known restrictions and wanted to go exploring the decks but his confidence was lacking. The pitch and heave of the ship now it was at sea frightened him and he crept into his bunk again. There was a fascinating new world to discover and it wasn't long before it had him out and about, unsure of himself at first, but then with growing confidence.

By the third day out the reserve of the passengers began to give way to a sense of conviviality that slowly weakened Hayward's fears. There were farmers, carpenters, fishermen, layabouts, pickpockets, flim-flam men, soldiers and some recently released from Debtors prison and workhouse's. There was little to do but talk and Hayward learned avidly. He learned to play Whist, Poker and Penny-Farthing. At night he would curl up under his duffel coat, full of wonder at his good fortune.

Even the rock-hard biscuits, bean and pea swills and old salt meat made a welcome change. He hadn't eaten as well for years.

Awed, amazed, sometimes fascinated or occasionally jubilant Hayward began to forget the past.

The spells on deck were like holidays. He watched the workings of the ship with interest and came to know the meaning of the boson's orders bellowed out against the wind. The ocean amazed him. He had no notion before of its vastness. The Captain who read from the Bible on Sundays seemed to him to be a God. He was a stalwart man with a fine growth of whiskers and a manner of humble power.

Going before a good wind, he loved to hear the whiffle of the bow wave, the straining and creaking spars and the wind singing in the rigging. He marvelled at the wonder of ships harnessing the wind. Or in the Doldrums, when the sails flapped and crackled and the blocks clattered and the ship rolled in the swell, he listened to the sailors talk as they worked on sail or rope. The sun beat down on a steamy ocean and the ship heaved sickly or drifted on fitful and vagrant currents, the hazy sun blazing now abeam, now aft as the ship spun and rolled sluggishly on the glassy sea. Some boobies huddled on the spars looking glum, beaks open in the heat. People lay stupefied below or attempted some relief on deck but there was little to be found so that some were near madness, until without a breath of wind, rain poured down for an entire night, leaving strange sea-creatures on the deck and straggles of seaweed on the rigging. Hayward suffered with the rest, though it was all a wonder to him.

Then gusty puffs of cooler air began to promise a change, along with a different look to the sea; there were little waves from the north by east and slowly the ship began to gather way. By the next morning the whole mood aboard had changed as the bow began to cut the water and the ship heeled to the wind.

When he felt the warmth of the southern sun and looked out to sea, bright and clean and good as nothing he had ever seen before, his spirits rose to feelings of freedom and joy he imagined the Albatross felt, flying free from ocean to ocean. Slowly, the grey burden of a mind that knew little reason for joy blew away in the salt breezes, the sky and the vast ocean.

Two days out from the Rio the ague struck. Men lay groaning and tossing. Others sat by them bathing their sweating foreheads with old rags. The Doctor was a very busy man. There was trouble in the other holds as well. He could do little anyhow, administering Laudanum as often as he could, or blankets for the freezing fevers. Two men died. The old hands feared typhus or cholera but this was something different. Apart from a few days of severe nausea that filled him with dread of never seeing his new land, Hayward was unaffected.

Life changed for them all, crew included, when the ship went south into the roaring forties. The winds howled, some seas seemed to tower above the masts and the ship rolled and tossed under furled sails. Two helmsmen roped to the wheel, seaboots, oilskins and sou'westers drenched with rain and sea water, fought to keep the ship out of trouble and heading east. The little ship, surging and plowing through the raging waters seemed encased in a deadly grey cocoon of tumult. After an adventurous passenger was washed overboard when a heavy sea crashed down upon the decks and the hold was awash with salt sea swill, the Master battened down the hatches and all below stayed in their bunks in the stinking dark. Some groaned, others prayed or spewed, some bold souls sang bawdy songs. Hayward, holding tightly to the edges of his bunk, had no doubt his end had come. After they were able to go on deck Hayward heard a sailor who had suffered three broken fingers and a head wound from a flying block, up aloft in the forties, tell a mate, "Any fool that goes to sea for pleasure would be fool enough to go to hell for a holiday."

As the ship left the forties and tacked northward the cold eased and they had some good days of sailing. No land was sighted after leaving Rio until the cry went up one afternoon. The ship was abuzz with expectation within seconds. Every passenger wanted to go aloft to see the new land but were restrained until the ship anchored in the Swan River. They were then marshalled up on deck to look at it. They were all aghast at the dreary spectacle of barren sand with not a tree in sight. The only evidence of civilization was a flagpole, a straggle of simple houses and scattered tents. All took heart when the Master yelled, "This is not where yer going. Cheer up! Port Jackson's a long way off yet!"

"Is this not Australia then?" Hayward asked a seaman.

"Tis to be sure. This here settlement is scarce ten year old, m' boy. Port Jackson's way over on the east coast. You're in for some heavy seas yet across the Bight afore we be coastin' north. We'll be here for a few days victualing up but you immigrants won't get shore leave. You'll be sick enough of staring afore then."

For the next hour they all stood on deck talking about this strange place they had come to. All they knew about their new land was hearsay. True to the sailor's word great swells and high winds buffeted the ship when they entered the Great Australian Bight. The deck was awash so they stayed below having a merry time singing to a seaman's harmonium, telling stories, playing cards and dancing whenever the ship stopped rocking and pitching. Hayward had sung hymns on Sundays in the workhouse but this was the first time he sang with joy. As soon as the weather cleared they stormed up on deck trying to catch sight of the coast.

As they neared Port Jackson there was much talk amongst them. Apprehensions, speculations, and trepidations were confessed and misinformation exchanged. The tension increased as they sailed north.

By the time they hove-to well out from the cliffs forming the headlands to Port Jackson excitement ran high. When the Captain gave the vessel over to the harbor pilot he called for the passengers to come on deck for a look at what he called 'the finest harbor in all the world'.

It was a fine, if gusty, winter morning, the breeze keen. Not one person, save the sailors, had ever seen such sights. They stood grasping rigging or rails watching in awed silence as the ship moved slowly down the harbor. To one side, wooded bluffs and sandstone fore shores and shallow cliffs dropping to breakers, to the other, the green paddocks of Watsons Bay, fishermen's huts behind bright little beaches the color of apricots lapped by little waves of the clearest blue. Beaches, inlets and bays passed slowly, some with vales on which crops grew or animals grazed, above them wooded hills with a house or road visible through the trees. Across the harbor the forest grew down to the rocks and low cliffs without a house or road to be seen. One of them cried out "Savages! Look there!" pointing to three blacks standing in the shallows, spear arm raised, triple barbed spears close to the surface. They were so intent they ignored the passing ship but the passengers rushed to get a sighting. As they looked towards the southern shore, bays and coves passed with more evidence of habitation. There was much pointing and shouting as one or the other spotted a windmill, house or boat shed as they neared Farm Cove.

Restlessness went through them all. They looked at each other with surreptitious smiles. The wonder of these sights and the release of knowing the tedious passage was ending were too much and someone cried out "Three Cheers!" Others followed. One cried "Hip hip! And the rest bellowed out "Hooray!" Three times, "hip hip – hooray!" sounded out over the water, each shout louder and longer than the last. They shook hands or embraced each other, couples feeling free to do so for the first time since leaving Liverpool.

Friends slapped Hayward on the back saying, "Well mate, you're here! How goes it with you?" but Hayward was too bemused and excited to answer. His throat was tight and there were hot tears in his eyes.

After the Stafford was rowed into a small bay, the anchor was dropped and preparations for disembarking were begun. All in all it had been a good passage. There had been only one stabbing and five deaths.

The officers were busy getting the passengers to form two lines from the bulwarks down to the holds or supervising their descent into lighters. Spirits ran high that morning, spilling over into brave talk and sudden friendships, though some were silent with relief or apprehension for such as it was, the Stafford had been home to them for a long time.

Hayward was one of the silent ones. He was too busy soaking everything up; the blueness of the water; the silver shine of the bright sun upon it; the tones of the sandstone edging the shore, the strange trees every color but green.

There was no wind now. The sea was flat with calm. As he sat in the lighter, his bundle on his knees, he could see a pleasant vale with huts and a house or two surrounded by rows of a tall plant he could not recognize with other growing things as well as penned sheep and goats. It looked so calm and ordered in the bright warm sun. 'For all I know' he thought, 'that might be where I am going!'

The oars dipped silently into the water. There was no sound but the slow rhythmic creak of the rowlocks. There was little talk even as they clambered onto a low wharf and stood milling about looking for friends or family or studying the landscape.

Not far in-shore Hayward could see a large square building of white washed stone with a large forecourt, on each side long sheds of roughly adzed timber with roofs jutting out far past the walls. Behind were rows of tents.

Two soldiers marched out of the building towards them. One was an officer. He bellowed "Immigrants, attention!" In a voice that could be heard on the north shore.

He shouted "Welcome" at them. "Now then, you wonder where you are. Sydney Town is over yonder. You'll be billeted here for a day or so until you're hired out. Married men with wives aboard file out to yonder barracks. All others march off to the tents. Follow my man here."

This was the first strangeness the immigrants were to find. Friendliness and informality from adults in authority was new to them and so was his unusual way of speaking.

Carrying a very odd assortment of bags and boxes, they were marched to the tents. At each one they were sloped off in pairs until every man was billeted.

Hayward sat down on a canvas stretcher and looked at his tent-mate. He had seen him on deck occasionally but had not got to know him because they were from different holds. His small eyes had a whimsical look pronounced by thin, angled eyebrows like the gables of a roof. This gave him a humorous, quizzical look. Hair grew wispy about his ears and down the back of his head but his crown was bald and mottled. Two deep lines ran from the sides of his nose and disappeared under an unkempt beard.

Sitting knees high in the sag of the canvas stretcher they looked at each other. The little man cocked an angled brow and winked the other eye.

"Tis a rum go it be," he said. "A rum go. Well me young shaver, seein' as 'ow we got tented together and like as not will be a day or so, me name is Edward Everett Ramsey, called Ted."

"Good morning, Mr Ramsey sir" Hayward responded. "I'm Hayward Redstone."

Mr Ramsey cocked both eyebrows.

"Smartly said young shaver-me-lad, but you best call me Ted". His brows sagged as he looked disconsolately about the tent. "What now? What now? Six months from home I be lad, now sitting here at the bottom of the world and the Devil knows if we shall ever see home again, nor wots to become of us."

"Yes, sir," Hayward agreed

Edward Everett Ramsey lay down. Deep in his canvas cradle he continued, "I'd like as not change places with a young blood as you be, right enough. Smart of brain and strong of limb I wager. As for me you could say I'm a mite long in the tooth eh? Now here I be, a self-taught man. Bettered myself I did with a little good luck and hard trying. I'm a bookbinder by trade and miss the smell o' glue. Don't expect much in that line".

He sat up and looked out through the tent-flap.

"Now here's a soul wots been off ship no more'n two hours in this New South bloody Wales and I'm sure unhappy with the place."

Incredulous at this statement Hayward asked, "Why, how can that be, not taking to our new country so soon?"

"Not right off I don't. No sir not right off. Likely I'll get used to it as I have to, but it's too hot an' bright out there for the likes o' me, and too much space between things like. So I'm thinkin' the cot's the place f'r me. But you're a young blood an'll want to make out and about. So off y' be Hay and tell me of it."

The morning boat ride with its sights, the friendly officer with his bland way of speaking, the warm sun, the spicy smell of land all contributed to Hayward's feelings of wellbeing. Everything seemed marvelous and intriguing. Most of the men were out looking about or talking in small groups. Many men greeted him with, "Mornin' lad", or "Here at last! You faring well?"

The following morning the assignments began. Freemen and emancipates, the landed gentry of the New South Wales Corps, squatters and settlers, merchants and tradesmen of all kinds, desperate for workers, were punted across the narrows to check the lists of immigrants and their particulars.

Mr Ramsey felt vulnerable, thinking that he would be little use to any.

"Hay m' lad, I'm thinkin' it would be good if we teamed up like. Y' see I'm feelin' the need of a stout friend. What do y' say?"

"Well, I think I would like that Mr Ramsey, 'cause I'm not knowing but I don't see how that's possible."

"Well let say I be your kin. Cousins like. The son of your mother's eldest sister, an' if we vouch for each other it might just work."

"So it might!" Hayward said, "well Mr Ramsey it won't hurt to try and if it pleases you it is all right by me."

"Capital! Cousins then!" And they shook on it.

And so it was that they were both assigned to one George Arthur Sorrel, son of a first-fleeter, by his friend and agent William Falkner Pascoe, merchant, of Parramatta Town. They signed their papers of release and assignment and led by the portly Mr Pascoe, were taken across the narrows to a horse and cart driven by a surly man who wore a blouse and sailor's pants but no shoes. Mr Ramsey nudged Hayward and cocked a brow at the sight. Mr Pascoe climbed with difficulty into a sulky and drove off, the cart lumbering along behind.

They skirted the farm Hayward had seen, passed some black fellows sitting in the dust, dressed in rags and drinking from bottles, climbed a ridge and passed into Sydney Town. Their feelings flowed now this way and that like sea in the scuppers,. Mr Ramsey sat hunched, eyes screwed up against the light, muttering, "By all that's holy, It's a rum place."

When he saw a man with fine shiny shoes, tight pants to the heel, braces over a collarless shirt, sleeves rolled up and no jacket at all, walking down the street smoking a cigar he said, "Did a man ever see the likes?" Hayward grinned. He enjoyed having Mr Ramsey along.

They were both intrigued with new sights, while the surly man sat hunched at the reins in a doze.

"Not a cobble to be seen!" said Mr Ramsey.

A flash cove dressed in a blouse and brightly patterned waist coat, knee boots over moleskin pants, wide blue velvet ribbons flowing off his cabbage tree hat, rode past on a cob. As he passed he called out, "G'day gentlemen!" The two immigrants looked at each other in surprise.

"Well I never...!" said Mr Ramsey.

They passed many building sites where masons were busy hewing and dressing stone. They saw soldiers standing guard over laboring convicts and passed white stucco houses with pig pens or fowl pens behind them. There were many inns with men in shirt sleeves sitting outside drinking and an amazing assortment of people in strange dress going about their business.

They saw three horsemen, tanned and lean, in open shirts with neckerchiefs, bright waistcoats, and spurred knee boots. One wore a holster off a wide belt; another had a pistol sticking out of a scarlet sash. Their saddles hung with saddlebags, tuckerbags and bedrolls. They filled Hayward's heart with envy and longing. He determined that one day, he too would look that that.

The cart rattled over a little bridge across a trickle of water in a gully and headed for the harbor. Ships lined each side of a small cove. Transports, whalers and coasters were anchored out in the harbor.

"I'm afeared o' what's coming next I am, youngen" Mr Ramsey confessed.

The surly man heard. Turning about he said in that flat tone they thought so strange, "It's a trip up the coast for you two new chums. Stone the bloody crows, afeared ya be already! Wait till Captain Smollet lets loose on ya." He turned back laughing.

"Oh no! We're for the sea again" Mr Ramsey wailed. "God damn it but I sure wish meself back t' the smell o' the Thames. Back in the factory would suit me fine."

"Come on Ted, cheer up. All will be well, believe me." Hayward told him. There was wonder in his eyes and a happy smile on his lips and a young man's optimism shining in his voice.

"Right you are youngen. Right enough f'r you pr'aps but I'm dizzy as a man rolling downhill in a barrel Likely I'll get used to it in a year or two."

Hayward gave him a slap on the back. "A day or two more like!"

The cart rumbled to a stop. They were at a wharf. A spanking new brig lay alongside with Mr Pascoe standing aboard waiting.

"There yar. Sight seein' trip's over. Hop down" The man said.

"Come aboard. Take care on the plank," called Mr Pascoe from the taffrail. Turning to another man he said, "Take these two to the cuddy, Mr Mate. Give them tea and some Johnny cakes while I talk with the Captain"

"G'day youse blokes. Ow ya goin'? Good passage? A bit more t' go, ay? No sweat, you'll be on the Yarrandabbie afore the weeks out. Come amidships." He ushered them into the cuddy and sat them down. "Take the weight off. I'll duck into the galley and get yer a cuppa."

"Struth" Mr Ramsey said, "I can't make 'ead nor tail of wot that man says."

"Neither can I. But I reckon we're in for a cup of tea anyway."

The mate came in with two tin mugs of black tea and a plate of small round cakes.

"Neat little craft ay? She's a humdinger. Proud to be Mate. Pascoe an' Sorrel 'ad 'er built at Port Macquarie. We sails up an' down 'tween settlements an' Sydney. Supplies on the way up, timber and produce on the way down. Grouse, ay? Me moniker's Bert, wots yours? Wots yer trade?"

Grateful to get a word in Mr Ramsey said, "Me name's Ted an' this 'ere's Hayward, me cousin on 'is mother's side. I used to be in the bookbinding business an..."

Hayward cut in with "And I'm a young adventurer!" He glowed with pride that this was true. He was no longer a blacker-boy in a workhouse. He was sure he would never be so lowly again.

"Well now, ain't that grand. Gawd only knows wot adventures you'll be 'avin up at Sorrel's place on the Yarrandabbie. Timber cutter, snigger, sawyer, shepherd, stockman, plowboy...Gawd knows. About the only adventure you'll be getting is if you're game to go into the settlement on yer day off. If yer gets one that is." He saw Mr Pascoe on his way down from the skipper's cabin. "Smarten up! 'ere comes the boss."

"All right Bert, go about your business" Mr Pascoe said, adding, "Talk the leg off an iron pot he will". He lowered his ample backside onto a stool.

"Now then. We've had a few workers from the immigration scheme before, Mr Sorrel and I, and I'm bound to say we have been none too pleased...A scivvy made off at week's end with one of the shepherds, and another was a lay-about that needed the whip, and another stole Mr Sorrel's pistol and shot himself dead. Now I see before me two likely looking lads." - He cast a doubtful look at Mr Ramsey – "And I'm bound to tell you on behalf of Mr Sorrel that there's none fairer on the whole stretch of the Yarrandabbie. The whole coast for that matter. You'll do well by doing well by him.

"As from today you are in the employ of the same, so you'll answer to Captain Smollet and be doing as he says as Mr Sorrel has an interest in this craft. You'll get three good meals a day, quarters, and wages of twenty pounds a year and there's many as would say it's too grand seeing as you are new chums and as good as useless. Life in the bush is another thing. Another thing entirely. So keep your weather eye open, do as you're told and learn fast." Mr Pascoe took his watch chain from his fob pocket, opened his silver watch, put on his specs and read the time.

"Now I must be off. Take heed of Captain Smollet mind – he'll be down to speak to you presently. Good day." He waddled out.

They looked at each other. "Crikey! Did you hear that Ted? Twenty pounds a year! And our keep!"

"And maybe the whip too by the sounds of it," said Mr Ramsey with a doleful air.

"No surely not. They all seem fine folk and Mr Pascoe spoke highly of Mr Sorrel"

They heard a shout. "You two bondsmen look alive now! Present yourselves aft."

"That must be us," said Hayward.

They left the cuddy and looking aft saw a stocky man in a black frock coat standing at the taffrail, hands behind his back, rocking slowly from heel to toe. An immense beard hid his face. Two burning eyes looked out from under a black peaked cap.

"Gawd," said Mr Ramsey under his breath.

"I'm Mr Smollet, the Captain of this craft and ye'll address me as such". His burning eyes looked from one to the other. 'I'm a God fearing man and a good Protestant by the blessed will o' God. I hope to heaven there are no Papists here!"

"Not I," volunteered Mr Ramsey.

Hayward, a little confused by the turn of events said, "I'm Church of England." Though he wasn't really sure.

"Humph," said Captain Smollet, "a mixed blessing. Now you two, know any sea craft? No? Well you'll learn a bit on the way up. You're not passengers but deck hands so do as you're told by the mate, Mr Metz and the bo'sun.

"Now I'm bound to warn you for the saving of your immortal souls that without the Good Book and a contrite heart you'll go to perdition in these colonies. Sydney Town is a sewer of perfidity. A sewer I say! And you can thank God you'll not be going ashore again. The settlements are little better. Debauchery, living in sin, drunkenness, and lechery everywhere. Mark my words you're in mortal danger." He cast his eyes heavenward and cried, "Lord protect these two men from the terrible temptations to mortal sinning and the everlasting hellfire that follows! Amen."

"There now. Nothing here is like it is at home so tread carefully. Have nothing to do with any Papist nor the black heathen lest they be Christened and chastened and then take care for there are none like them as touches upon perfidity, slovenliness, abominations, and pernicousness!"

Feeling his duty done, he touched his brow with a slight nod of this head and strode off to his cabin.

The two penitents, sobered by the Captain's sincerity and fervor, stood staring ahead. They felt sheepish and unsure what to do next, until Bert arrived from the focsle.

"You've been told and warned, eh?" He laughed. "Well, me hearties, there's plenty more where that come from. The old man's full of it. Get your bundles and come below."

There were eight bunks in the focsle.

"Take your pick of any as long as they're these two," Bert laughed. "Stow your bundles in this here locker. Daily gear in nets above yer head. Strip to blouse and strides and come topside."

The Captain's harangue caused a flicker of old trepidations for Hayward.

"That bloody skipper right puts the wind up me," Mr Ramsey told Hayward in a whisper.

"He reminds me of one or two I'd best forget. But it'll only be for a week or so an' we'll be ashore."

Up on deck they ran into trouble with the bosun.

"Strike a light! Look at these two greenun's! Get yerselves below an' bare yer bloody toes," he roared. The crew on watch laughed but it seemed to Hayward that it was in good spirit.

They soon found that the bosun was a friendly man. He gave them only light duties and took pains to see they understood the workings of the ship. That night they ate lamb chump chops with cabbage, peas and beans, fresh bread and butter and strong tea. Hayward climbed into his bunk with a light heart. It was the first time he had eaten lamb. It was the best meal he had ever eaten. His bunk had a blanket and a heavy linen sheet; even a pillow!

Bert awakened them before dawn to prayers for a good passage as they did every morning after. As many of the crew as possible stood before the Captain while he shouted, "Lord, see to it that this passage is a good one. Protect us from the fury of the elements and render them clement. Protect these, my charges, from the temptations of the flesh in the settlements and bless this ship in the name of Christ. Amen. Now to work!"

Sailing up the harbor was a marvelous experience. The morning was bright with a fresh south wind, cold in the dawn light. Captain Smollet was at the wheel dressed in a black frock coat with silver buttons, black trousers with a grey stripe down the sides, and a black peaked cap. Mr Metz stood by for orders though none were given. Under light sail the brig tacked out through the heads, northing into the open sea.

"Excellent wind, Mr Metz. Take the wheel and send the men aloft." Captain Smollet went below.

The mate called, "All sail aloft bosun."

The bosun blew his whistle and assigned each man his task. It was not long before the ship heeled, surging north under the southerly.

"Hay! Go aloft and see how it's done. Are ya game o' heights?" The bosun asked.

"I think so sir. I sure hope so."

"You there, Hans, take this young shaver aloft and show him the ropes."

He had wanted to do this for months. Excited with the prospect but nervous with fears, he waited for Hans to mount the ratlines.

"The tricky bit is getting' onto the lines" Hans affirmed. "Grab them high one handed, mount the bulwark, grab with the other hand an' up ya go!"

Hayward knew exactly what to do. He had marveled at the sailor's alacrity on board the Stafford and had rehearsed the mounting in his head many times.

"Bloody great!" said Hans as he moved to one side to let Hayward go first.

"Elbows out! Keep yer body tight in! Not too fast now. No leaning sideways. Watch yer mitts. Yer feet'll know where to go."

Being aloft was the most marvelous experience of his life. He was exultant. He stood with an arm embracing the mast, the other grasping a shroud. There was little else but space about him. The vast dome was empty of cloud. The sea was dark blue with bright whitecaps chasing each other northward to the horizon, forward and starboard. To port, seas crashed violently against mighty cliffs, throwing spray high into the air with a muted roar. The rigging sung in whistles and shrieks and his hair blew about in merry confusion.

Being aloft sung in his soul the entire day as he swabbed the decks, cleaned the focsle, washed up and worked for the cook. Going well before the wind there was little to do aloft and time to linger about the deck watching the shoreline when it loomed in view.

The wind died then blew in restless gusts from every quarter. Before them and against them they battled their way up the sparsely settled coast, putting in at Newcastle and Port Stephens, unloading sugar, flour, tea and tools. There was little time in the Captain's tight schedule for the crew to sample the temptations they looked forward to. They saw Captain Smollet talking with Bert against the taffrail about purple cloud coming up from the south. Misty, darker streaks fell from them to the horizon. They heard Bert say, "Aye aye, Cap'n." Passing them, he said, "Squalls on the way. You land lubbers best go below."

"Could I stay on deck, Bert?" Hayward asked hopefully. He didn't want to miss out on another experience.

"I suppose so, as long as you stay belayed to the mast. You ain't got the sea legs for it."

"You're welcome to it youngen. I'm off!" Mr Ramsey said scuttling for the cuddy.

All was quiet. The wind died and the seas dropped. Nothing seemed to be happening and Hayward began wondering what a squall was. Even Mr Ramsey could be seen poking his head out to find out what it was all about.

A quarter hour later the Captain came on deck in a oilskin and sou'wester. The brig was sailing sluggishly, the Captain waiting, hands on the taffrail leaning towards the oncoming storm, keeping his weather eye open.

The wind freshened, then dropped. Light faded as the cloud descended. The sea was the color of mulberries. The wind changed, blowing steadily from the south in small gusts.

Captain Smollet turned. "Mr Mate! Drop the spanker! Reef the topsails."

He stood hands behind his back, knees slightly bent, taking the kick and surge of the craft, mind in the sails and wind.

"Take the helm Greer!" He roared. Greer was a short powerful man, good on a heavy helm. There followed a hiss of rain on the sea, obliterated by the sound of the gusts that hit the little ship and the pounding of wind-driven rain on the decks.

Captain Smollet put his Mackintosh collar up and roared in to the wind, "Let us have it Lord!"

And to the helmsman, as following seas swamped the decks "Ease her off a few points. Don't let us be pooped!" .

The crew took shelter in the cuddy, leaving Captain Smollet and Bert standing braced against the rail calling orders to the helmsman. Hayward was the only other on deck happily drenched, sitting with legs wrapped around the mast and enjoying seeing it all. He could feel the exultation of Captain Smollet joyously going before the blow, calling upon the Lord, the knowledge of his brig and his mastery of it.

Greer grappled with the helm as the seas and winds hit, sometimes embracing it, arms over, giving it his full body weight. Blocks rattled, sails cracked, the sea hissed, beat and gurgled over the deck and frothed in the scuppers, wind whistled and screeched in the rigging as the small brig, in her element, rode the tumultuous seas.

As if turned off by tap the rain stopped. The following wind dropped, then changed quarters. The brig sank down into a strange quietness as the crew waited for orders.

"All sail aloft! Put her to Port. Hold course till you sight land." And as the Mate passed, "A fine blow, Mr Mate!"

Northward they sailed. More often than not, Ted and Hayward were incredulous at the sights they saw. Small green islands ringed with white in an azure sea; wooded mountains rising up from the shore, mile after mile of beach curved between treed or grassy headlands; high sand hills and dense scrub, rocky points, and as they got further north, wild natives on the beaches and headlands and the smoke of their fires rising.

Then late one afternoon the call came from aloft," Hat Head a comin' up!"

Captain Smollet came on deck, looking at it with satisfaction.

"A good run," he said to Bert, then looking out to sea and the sky in all quarters, "This'll hold Mr Metz. Fly the main jib and we'll round Smokey Cape and have the pick down by dusk."

They passed the Cape and its island, rounded a northerly promontory and anchored in a wide bay.

The bay was so protected there was no surf on the beach, which curved in a beautiful arc to a low rocky point, then the beach curved again far north to a high headland rising abruptly from the sea.

Bert told them, "See those rocks jutting out from yonder hill? River's this side. T'morra, the weather bein' right, we'll warp our way in on the tide."

Hayward was given the dog watch at anchor, giving him a welcome opportunity to see and feel the land. It was quiet as the sun set. The sky was a darkening blue. There were huge clouds rising out of the land, towering up to sunlit curves, shining white. In the lee shore the shallow water was as smooth as a piece of yellow silk, glowing from bright green to blue as it got deeper. It slowly lapped the beach with minute waves. Groups of gulls and terns preened themselves on the beach. A pelican soared down over the trees from behind the dunes, angling its wing-beats to slow its sailing bulk, ski to a halt on its webbed feet, and then ride languorously on the still water. Dolphins came to play, but bored with the stillness of the ship, sped off broaching in unison.

Seaward, an albatross, symbol of his aspirations, rode the air with majestic ease. The last of the day's light shone on the headland scrub. Tones of grey, silver, olive and blue-green danced off the leaves. The far curve of shore became mysterious in shadow, sombre and dark. The silence was deep, amplified, not interrupted, by the gentle sounds of water lapping and the distant call of gulls. Day slipped silently into night.

The old desperation and hopelessness were forgotten as the sense of wonder and delight became as familiar to him as the feeling of drudgery used to be. He had changed so much, though he had not realized it. He had filled out, the pallor had gone. He stood straight and moved with confidence. The way he spoke was slowly changing as well. There were fewer deferences in his tone and he said few 'sir's' nor tugged a forelock. Without knowing it, he was slowly starting to become more like a currency lad. And a man.

Mr Ramsey came on deck, munching an apple. "Tricks up. There's stew on. But look here Hay, afore yer go below I'm wonderin' how all this strikes yer. I'm fair getting a fit o' the willies. I reckon there's a heap o' nothing in this 'ere New South Wales and we're in for a right crook time. I seen nothin' but a few savages since we left Port Macquarie. An' there weren't much to talk of there. Mark my words Hay, there'll be no pub an' snug nor easy women, or pie shops, hangin's to watch or anything much to watch at all in this here huge tangle o' forest. I'm tellin' yer, if I had the guts I'd do a bolt."

This confession sobered Hayward with intimations of reality. He looked at his bare toes.

"Jeesus Ted," he said slowly, "I've had a grand time these last few hours but you've put a damper on it." He looked into those bright little eyes under a furrowed brow. "But I know how yer feel. Maybe I'm just sick o' frettin' but I ain't a'feared anymore. We made our bed so now we gotta lie in it come what may. All these blokes are right prime if you ask me an' so long as Sorrel's blokes are half as cheery, what's to fear? And look 'ere, Ted, who said there's no pub or a bit o' funnin'? There's bound to be a bit of a settlement we can make to once in a while."

"Yeah s'pose yer right. Oh well..." He strolled away and sat on a barrel looking into the darkness.

Early next day, as the tide began to flow, Captain Smollet tacked towards the river mouth under light sail. "Drop the sheet anchor and float the pinnace." He called as they hove-to out from the river mouth. The tedious process of warping the ship into the river kept all hands busy for the next few hours. They rested, chatting, telling yarns and smoking while they waited for a wind from seaward. It started to blow, as it usually did, early in the afternoon.

"Up anchor! Break out the tops'ls Mr Metz," the Captain called, taking the wheel, cautiously putting the brig up the river.

The crew lounged below or sat about the deck yarning, splicing rope and tending sails.

Hayward and Mr Ramsey were intent on watching the banks in silent wonder. Once past the islands surrounded with mangroves the forest grew to the water. Timber getters had felled the cedar and rosewood but there were stands of huge hardwoods, palms and many other trees in a dense tangle of vines.

"Gawd but it's dark in there" said Mr Ramsey. "I once saw book pictures like that and there were tigers and monstrous bears and snakes big around as me thigh. Wot's a man t' do if 'e runs into the likes o' them I wonder."

"Remember them blokes we saw in Sydney? Why, you carry a pistol in yer belt, that's wot yer do!"

"Oh God struth Hay! W'ere we goin' to get a ruddy pistol from?"

"Maybe yer get's em with the job."

"Look 'ere you new chums, pistols nor muskets no use with these 'ere tigers. Takes a canon t' stop 'em it does. Cause there's no good troublin' yerself if it's the snake as got yer. Wrap yer up firearm an' all. One squeeze an' yer pulp! An' the bears, why, they drop outa the trees on yer afore yer knows it. If yer smart yer wanta remember t' always carry a pocket full of black pepper with yer. Black pepper mind, not white. It's the one thing those jungle critters can't stand," Hans told them.

Cockatoos screeched. "My Gawd did yer get a load o' that racket." Mr Ramsey complained. "That's to be taken for birdsong in this 'ere New South bloody Wales I s'pose." Then with a sniffle and a twitch of the brows, "T'be expected, t'be expected…"

Parrots of all colors flew across the river in noisy flocks. Many different pigeons fed high in the trees. Kingfishers and finches darted in the vines and undergrowth. When whipbirds cracked Mr Ramsey gave a start but suppressed a comment. When kookaburras cackled he was speechless.

They were full of questions to which the crew responded with marvelous lies, a favorite sport with new chums.

"Let's go aloft for a better view!" said Hayward, mounting the bulwark. Mr Ramsey went no further but stood with one foot on the ratlines. Hayward mounted to the crow's nest and joined Fred Greer who was watching for floatage. From up there he could see the wide river narrowing through bights and reaches. The flat country extended as far as he could see but becoming less so as the river meandered up the valley. Not far ahead there were a few small hills, and in the far distance, mountains under a westering sun.

"Big valley ay?" said Fred.

"But this must be the biggest valley in the whole world!" said Hayward, who had never seen a small one.

"What does that yonder be?"

"Sugarcane. That's part of Sorrels holding, that is. We're nearly there."

"Avast there! By thunder, did I order those immigrants aloft? Get them off the shrouds, Mr Mate!" roared Captain Smollet.

From the bowsprit now, Hayward sat watching for signs of habitation. There was no forest along the southern waterline now, it being cleared of most of the big trees. Those that remained were dead. It was a dreary sight to see a forest of dead, grey, leafless trees. It affected them both.

"Did a man ever see such a dismal sight in all the world. All the trees are dead! I wonder wot 'appened to 'em? Maybe there's a dreadful disease 'ere as likely as not."

"See all them dead trees? That's the dreaded stiffenin' blight. Strikes men an' horses an' kills 'em outright. Ya just goes stiff as a poker and dead as a doornail." Hans told them, not wasting an opportunity.

"I'm on t' you blokes. Yer great leg pullers. It's done on purpose I wager," said Hayward. He would do his share of ringbarking in the years to come.

They made into a long reach. Well ahead they could see a wharf and a shed surrounded by crops and back of that a treed hill with some sort of structure on it.

After the brig had been warped up to the wharf and the sails furled, Captain Smollet twice primed a huge horse pistol. The two shots rang out in echoes across the river startling the crows out of the trees and the galahs off the ground. As they flew to the trees on the opposite bank the crows cawed and the galahs screeched. Mr Ramsey put his fingers into his ears and grimaced.

" Ramsey and Redpath," Captain Smollet called, "This is your home port – go get your belongings and report aft."

"Well lads," he said, as they stood before him, "One of Sorrel's men will be down within the hour so you'll be out o' my care, God be praised. Take heed o' what I told ye mind, and take care o' your immortal souls. There are some as do well in this colony an' some as don't. If I be seeing you again I hope I can tell be the cut o' your jib as you've done the rightful and taken heed. Now help the crew unload and go ashore. Not out of sight o' the mast y' hear?"

"Aye aye, cap'n," they said like a pair of old salts.

Later they wandered about disconsolately waiting. By the wharf was a long shed of saplings roofed with slabs of bark where Sorrel's goods had been stacked. A wide track ran between stands of corn towards a small hill. Most the crew were washing clothes or trying out their land legs or their luck with fishing lines.

Mr Ramsey sidled up to Fred Greer, having a spell sitting on a barrel smoking his clay pipe.

'You know of George Sorrel, Fred?" He asked.

"Too right I do," Said Fred.

"Wot sort o' fella is 'e?"

"Sorrel? He's a devil of a man. Built like a brick dunny. He's powerful angry. Done a few blokes in I hear an' is ferocious with a stockwhip an'..." But he saw the dismal look on Mr Ramsey's face.

"Sure I'm only pullin' yer leg, Ted. Don't you worry, he's a grand bloke. Tough though. But who coulda done wot e' done without bein' rugged? He an' Duncan McLusky opened this country up. Pushed up from Port on a two-bullock slide and found the cedar stands and snigged 'em back two be two. The blacks did Duncan McLusky in first year, poor Scots bastard. Didn't stop George none. He had a few blacks on side by then an' felled the best o' the cedar afore the others were game enough t' give it a burl. He's claimed squatter's rights to the best land right up to Butcher's Creek an' done real well. A few years ago he got a missus from Port an' she's smartened 'im up no end I hear. 'E even built a house. But look 'ere Ted, no use pretendin' it's a bed a roses workin' on a holdin'. It's tough yakka. But George'll see to it you're not stretched. That young bloke'll get the rough end o' the pineapple I reckon. 'E can take it, see? That's George for ya. Great bloke."

Much relieved by this report, Mr Ramsey went to tell Hayward what he had found out, but was interrupted by a strange sound. "Gawd blimey wot was that?" he asked. The call was coming from inland somewhere. Fred put his hands to his cheeks and bellowed back, "Cooee!"

Then to Mr Ramsey, "Ere 'e comes now."

Turning around they saw another strange sight. Two red bullocks were pulling a large flat piece of timber mounted on slides like the bearings of a sledge. Along its sides slight timbers fenced it about except for the end, which had a high ridge across it. The two bondsmen saw George Sorrel for the first time, walking alongside leading the bullocks by a nose rope.

They were impressed. Sorrel was at least six feet tall Hayward judged, broad but lean. He walked loosely but with a slight stoop. He wore a blouse without sleeves revealing brown, well-muscled arms. He wore a cabbage tree hat and very soiled moleskins kept up with a plaited thong. He was waving.

"Fred, that couldn't be him, surely!"

"My colonial oath it is," Fred said, waving back.

They watched as he sauntered down the track with the lumbering bullocks.

Captain Smollet had heard the call and came onto the wharf.

"Greetings George!" he called, waving.

George said nothing until he too was on the wharf.

"G'day Captain Smollet. These the blokes?" – nodding towards Hayward and Mr Ramsey.

"They are. You two! This is your boss George Sorrel. George, this is Edward Ramsey and the young lad is Hayward Redpath."

They were both taken aback when their boss said, "G'day. It'll be Ted an' Hay. I'm George but the missus likes the hands t' call me boss." And shook their hands.

Hay and Ted nodded and shuffled about.

"Load the slide an' stick about. I'll go below with the Captain a while."

Half an hour later he came down the gangplank.

"All loaded? Come on then."

Feeling very uncomfortable Hayward and Mr Ramsey followed the slide up the track. The sun was low on the western horizon, going down behind blue-black mountains. Colorful parrots gathered in the hundreds chattering loudly in the tree-tops. Frogs croaked in the creek. Thousands of flying foxes took to the skies. Kookaburras laughed the day to its end in an ancient family ritual. New to all these daily events they noted each new thing with interest, though old trepidations loomed on the fringes of their awareness. Nothing was said. They were on top of a rise when a black man came forward. It was hard for them both to look somewhere else. He was dressed like a white man though of poor standing, was as black as soot, had a huge nose across his face and his eyes were hidden in a black furrow.

"Oh my Gawd! Get an eye full ov wots commin' Hay – a savage in pants," whispered Mr Ramsey, leaning towards Hayward's ear.

"Well 'e can't be much of a savage if 'e's got pants on."

"But look at 'im! I wish I was back on the brig I do."

Close by they could see a house little more than a shanty. It had a fence around it protecting flowers, vegetables and fruit trees. It was one of the few sights to earn the approval of Mr Ramsey since he left the Mother Country.

"You two this is Pumpkin. Pumpkin this is Ted an' Hay," the boss said, waving a big callused hand in their direction. "Stow the goods, Pumpkin. You two come in an meet the missus."

Mrs. Sorrel was a woman with a rather coarse face and unkempt hair, but a cheery manner.

Mr Sorrel said, "Here they are m'dear." And went out.

"Sit ya selves down, ya poor immigrants an' I'll make ya a cuppa," she announced, filling a teapot from a big iron fountain hanging over the fire in the hearth. She put the pot in a grid by the clay walls of the fireplace and said, "Now, while it's drawin' I've made some Johnny cakes for ya. Pass 'em 'round. Now wot are ya called?"

They introduced themselves but stood looking very awkward.

"Sit down, sit down why don'tcha? On the flitch there."

Had she not waved toward a narrow plank of timber on short legs they would not have known what she meant. With a handful of cakes they sat down and looked around, speechless. Mrs. Sorrel seemed not to mind as she prattled on about the drought, the crops, how much timber had been shipped last year, the problem with the betongs and bandicoots getting into her vegetables and local gossip. There was much she told them they could not understand. It made them both feel even more out of place.

England was as foreign to her as her world was to the Englishmen. Neither George nor Mrs. Sorrel ever asked what part of England they had come from or anything else about it. They had been born in the bush. England was not home to the Sorrels.

Hayward looked surreptitiously about the room. It smelt strongly of burnt wood and old ash. It was cluttered and untidy but though Mr Sorrel looked like a common worker he was obviously a rich man judging by the many things he owned. The hearth was big enough to roast a sheep in. The clay formed part of the end wall, running to the corners. The top of it was cluttered with things. There were pots and pans, mugs, pannikins and flatirons. Inside the fireplace chains hung down over the flames. From one the hot water fountain hung and from another a large oval pot with a heavy lid from which spurts of steam hissed.

Mrs. Sorrel took a fire tool and lifted the lid off, giving it a stir.

"Possum stew tonight," she told them proudly.

On the floor against the blackened clay were camp ovens and a small wooden bucket made from a barrel sawn in half, rigged with a rope handle. The big table was made of pit-sawn slabs roughly adzed. On top were crock-pots and a box of utensils, an oil lamp and a bowl with a pipe and a pack of Nigger's Twist tobacco in it. Two flitch benches were underneath it.

From the mantle hung toasting forks, poachers, tongs, tart molds and a wide mouthed hearth shovel with turned-up edges. In the middle was a huge brass bound mirror.

'So many things!' Hayward thought.

He did not notice the walls of rough hardwood planks all different colors and textures caulked with clay, nor the old canvas that sagged under the bark roof. He did not know that one of the sags was a ten-foot python snoozing snug in its winter quarters. There were too many other things to note and wonder about.

There was a large wooden seachest with a big bolt and padlock. One end was wedged to keep it level on the floor of pounded ashes. Hanging on the walls were three guns – later he would learn that one was a fowling piece, another a twelve-bore double barrel shot gun and a rifle. Two pistols hung from nails, along with a belt and clipped holster, hats, oilskins, a cutlass and coiled whips. A door in the corner led, Hayward suspected, to the bedroom.

For the first time since becoming cousins the two were thinking the same thoughts. Everything seemed so topsy-turvy in the colony. Fancy a rough worker like George Sorrel owning all this and stock and his own land and a share in the brig as well! He didn't look a day over thirty-five! And he had no airs and acted and spoke like one of them – nothing like a squire should. It was very perplexing. Sorrel came in.

"Give us a cuppa, love," he said, pulling a flitch out with his boot and sitting down. He spun his cabbage tree hat across the room to the top of the sea chest.

"Well, that's t'day just about done. I'm beat. Now you blokes, Pascoe had wised you up. You've a lot to learn an' we'll get stuck inta it t'morra. You, Ted, will bunk down in the lean-to as the missus'll be your boss more'n me. You Hay, will be headin' out to the fellin' and learn the axe. You can billet in me old hut. There's pannikins and mugs an' plates an' stuff there, cookin' things and a fireplace. Wen ya hears the missus strike the iron it's tucker time. You brings ya plate and pannikin up. 'Ow's the stew goin love?"

"Ready wen youse are George," she said.

"Ready? I've been ready since dinnerbloodytime. I could eat a horse and chase the jockey! Ted an' Hay, front up. Thora, give 'em a bowl an' spoon."

Little was said by the new chums during the meal, except "Yes'm, fancy! Really?"

Hayward was restless to ask what a possum stew was but thought better of it. He knew it was one of the many things he would learn in the days to come.

Over mugs of black tea after the meal, George told them thrilling stories of the early days until their heads swam with questions and adventure.

"Well, enough be o' yarnin' it's the kip for me an' the missus. Up with the kookas tomorra. Thora me love, if you show Ted his bunk I'll take the youngen t' the humpy. Better grab some candles Hay an' I'll take the lamp. Grab ya bundle."

George led the way through the garden gate, past the sheds and pens to a wattle and daub hut with a bark roof. The door was a slab of timber nailed to a post with leather hinges but it had a bolt on the inside.

"Hang on, I'll light a candle," George said, fumbling with the lamp. He lifted the chimney and lit the candle.

Hayward stood in wonder looking at his new home in the dim light of the oil lamp. There was a small table with a wash basin and jug, with drawers under it. Another had utensils strewn over it and a candle holder. An ant safe sat with its legs in a dish of water. The small fireplace and chimney were fashioned from tin sheets. There was a kettle and teapot on the hearth.

"Bed's on the other side of the hessian there." George said. "G'night, sleep tight. We'll rouse ya at sunup."

Hayward pushed the hessian aside to find an old metal bedstead on woodblocks. On it were a horsehair mattress and a rolled sheepskin pillow, a heavy linen sheet and wool blanket. A row of pegs was sunk into a beam at head-height. From one he hung his coat. He looked about again. He sat on the flitch at the table and tried the chair. He washed his face in the basin and wiped it on the hessian. He wanted to light a fire and sit by it and wonder but he knew it was too late for that. He thought with a thrill of anticipation, "Tomorrow maybe!" Knowing a strong delight, he sampled the bed. He lay in the blackness listening to the night sounds, too incredulous to sleep.

He thought, "This is my bed. This place is my home! Glory be!"

But the day had exhausted him. The wonder and excitement quickly faded into sleep.

THE SHINDIG

Bellinger River valley NSW 1842

A half-mile from camp Cliff Walsh put his calloused hands about his mouth and bellowed cooee! through his beard.

When the dray lumbered into camp Turnip came to help him unharness the bullocks.

"G'day Turnip" Cliff said. Looking around, he asked, 'Where's old Fred?"

'Ol' Fred, 'e unergroun'." Turnip said in a matter of fact tone.

"What? In the cellar?"

"No boss, unergroun' him bin now. Spider 'e jump up bite 'im bad. He bin in forest collectin' tucker. Bert boss he cuttem finger alongside an' suck, but Fred, 'e shake 'imself dead."

"Jeezus, another one! The poor old bugger. Grand old bushman he was. Everyone else hunky-dory?"

"All fella fine boss. That Major bloke an' 'is team bin commin' dinner along Christmas tucker time Hay tellem."

"What? You don't say! Well I'll be damned. Wonders never cease. Anyhow, it's time we had a bit of a shindig 'round here. What do you say to that Turnip?"

"My bloody colonial oath mine tinkit!" Turnip said with feeling. Cliff laughed.

"You would like that eh?"

"Too bloody right. Plurry good tucker bin commin' boss." Cliff laughed again.

He slapped the bullocks on the rump. "Go on, get!" he yelled.

By the time they had stowed the harness in the tack humpy and Turnip had made Cliff a pot of tea and found some oat cakes the rest of the blokes were dawdling into camp, axes and tucker bag over a shoulder. Hay and Ted were the last to arrive.

"G'day Cliff, back already? Good trip ay? Any trouble with the blacks?" Hay asked.

"Yeah it went real well. All the fords were low and it was too dry for mud an' I only saw one black. Old Mooloolah came into camp one night and scrounged a bit of tucker. Poor old bloke."

"Mooloolah, ay? Yes I remember him. He was one of the first we met when we came in about '39. He walks alone now. Did ya get all the stuff?"

"All but the chains. We're a few axe heads and dogs short. A few things are getting scarce down at the settlement. Captain Smollet reckons it'll be worth his while to test the bar when a few more squatters start producing crops. That'll be bonza, ay? Better light the lamps and get this stuff unloaded."

The men were like children about a Christmas tree. There was rum by the barrel and brandy for old Tom the cook, two hogsheads of beer for the Christmas shindig, boots and belts, moleskins, Mackintoshes, Carter's Little liver pills, Cayenne pepper and Senna pods (the bushman's cures 'for wot ever ails yer') and tins of Log cabin and packs of Nigger Twist tobacco. There were bottles of Goanna oil for the rheumatics, clove oil for the toothache, Soul's Salve guaranteed to heal any wound, Cooper's Dill water for the gripe and a stack of penny dreadfuls for the blokes that could read. Tom showed the two new blacks how to stow the provisions in tin trunks down in the cellar to keep them away from the critters while the men went to the river with towels and soap.

❧

By seven o'clock Christmas morning the two pigs had been slaughtered and bled. The men had built a large pit fire lined with stones. They rigged two spits over it. The roaring fire had died down to a ring of burning branches as thick as thighs out from the embers like spokes of a wheel.

Under Tom's direction, Turnip, Quartpot and Billy had fashioned a clay oven for baking bread, molded on lawyer vines. They used an old piece of sheet iron for a door. Providentially, the iron had a hole on one edge so they put this uppermost, tied a handle to it, and rested the base on two big stones each side of the fire.

Tom stood looking at it with a wrinkled brow. "Bloody lot of guess work going on here." he confided to himself. Tom admired his reputation as a bush cook and was out to impress that toff bloke and his team.

He stuffed his old cherrywood with Nigger's Twist and sat on a log puffing on the acrid smoke.

"Jeezus Tom, there's all this work t' do an' 'ere you are sittin' on your bloody blot smokin' f'r Chriz sakes. Shake a bloody leg there!" Hay had wrapped the big blocks of precious butter into wet canvass and was going into the cellar to hang them there.

"Look 'ere boss." Tom said, "I ain't doin' no loafin'. Fact is I'm wore out thinkin'. I'm not 'avin that bloody Major thinkin' old Tom's a colonial oaf wot can't bake bread an' burns a pie. No sir, I'm not 'avin it an' I'm sittin' 'ere a figerin' fire an' time an' weight so's I'll git it right first time."

"Bugger the bloody Major an' 'is team. Wot about us blokes?"

Tom puffed on, watching the oven like a fisherman watches his float. He knocked the dottle from his pipe on the heel of his boot and looked around. "Right Oh." He yelled, "You bloody niggers! Fetch the loaves an' bung 'em in the oven. You there, Quartpot, keep 'er stoked 'bout like she is. God damn it, did I say t' bring the pies? Turnip! Keep an eye on these blokes."

It was getting a bit too much for Tom. A man with his responsibilities could do with a refresher so he ducked down into the cellar and unearthed his bottle of Hospital Brandy from amongst the grain sacks and took a swig.

While down there he checked the number of Possum and Geebung pies just to be sure. There were corncobs and spuds wrapped in wet paper-bark to roast in the coals. "Oh my Gawd there's another thing a man's gotta git right." Tom remembered. Another swig was in order.

Fat began to drip from the pigs, hissing into the fire. Tom nailed a tin to a stick, gave it to Cliff and told him, "'Ere! Catch the fat in that. When it's full baste the bastards!"

Smoke built up under the tarp seeping out under the edges. "Tighten that bloody tarp why can't somebody?" Tom roared. "Baldy, cut a sapling and shove it under the tarp! For Chrize sakes can't you gormless coots git thet trestle even?"

Tom was having a marvelous time. He had a secret too, that he was tickled pink about. The day before Tom found a python curled up in one of the wagons and brought its life to an end with the aid of a nine-pound hammer. The men had commented on the skin, nailed to the side of the wagon. It was at least a foot wide and eleven feet long, but they didn't know that Tom had stuffed it into the pigs in neat rounds.

Tom was looking forward to the first bloke who asked what the delicious white meat was. He hoped it would be the Major because snake was nigger's food.

&sw;

About noon the Major's men arrived piled up in a dray with the Major alongside riding his bay stallion. Dressed in jodhpurs and leggings, pith helmet and a blouse with a yellow spotted bandana, the Major stood out like a sore thumb. His moustache had been treated with the last of his bandoline. He knew he was a formidable sight to these colonials but nevertheless he felt undressed because his big Colt-Paterson revolver in its clip-down holster was not on his belt. It was under the seat of the dray along with the other firearms.

The dogs made an impressive show of challenging the new-comers but quieted as Hay, coming forward, told them to lie down.

"Great! Glad you all could make it."

"Got one bloke down with colonial fever, otherwise we're all here," said the Major as he swung out of the saddle. "I guess this is the only Christmas celebration between the settlement and Brisbane."

"Yeh. Time to let bygones be bygones, eh, Major?"

The Major coughed. "Of course, of course," he said flatly. He started in surprise when Billy came up and spoke to him. "Take big fella horse along tucker, boss?"

"Lucerne, no oats," said the Major, letting the reins drop for Billy to pick up. Hayward's teeth clenched.

While they talked the men stood about with their panniken or pot in hand, the Major's men on one side, and Sorrel's men on the other. It looked like a standoff.

Like two armies drawn up to sign a truce the Major thought with a smile.

The men were so uncomfortable; Hayward could see a ca-tastrophe looming. It was up to him to take the reins in hand. Feeling a bit shaky he banged the tucker bell to get attention

"Ah...look you blokes, Major an' 'is men that is.. Wot I wanna say is, not only to the Major 'ere, but to all you codgers, well, we are all glad you're 'ere so welcome. Now Tom ... 'Ay there, where's Tom? Eh Tom!" Hayward looked about wishing he had decided against say anything.

Old Tom emerged from the pit cellar with a jar of his onion sauce in both hands.

"Stone the bloody crows, what now?" he complained.

"Now there 'e is! Come 'ere Tom!" He put his hand on Tom's shoulder. "This is the bloke we gotta thank f'r t'days tucker so give 'im a big 'and!"

The men clapped as ordered. Cliff and Oscar whistled. Bert shouted "Goodonya!" Baldy cried "Here here!"

"There's plenty of it so tuck in wen 'e gives the signal. Now where's that bloody keg?"

Hector and Oscar brought a keg out of the cellar, blocked it on the trestle, broached it and the men lined up to imbibe the much needed social lubricant.

All this onerous responsibility made Tom's heart pound with apprehension. The prestige of it made his mind swim. He barged about giving orders, elbowed his way between groups of men, moved things about on the trestle, or stood looking profoundly upon the pigs – and fortifying himself with a swig every time he went to the cellar.

A little bell rang amongst the clatter in his brain. The bread!

"Hey you! Turnip and Quartpot! Lift the flamin' door," he yelled, pointing to the oven while bustling for a long-handled shovel. He squatted to squint into the rosy glow. The six loaves looked like manna from heaven, beautifully risen, the tops a crusty brown.

"Stand back!" He ordered taking out each loaf on the shovel and putting them onto a spread copy of the Sydney Herald years old. The most marvellous smell wafted about so the hungry men came to admire the wonder of real yeast-risen, oven-baked bread.

"Easy-on!" Tom cried, "Stand away! It's gotta be slow-cooled!" He wrapped each loaf in a towel.

"There now," he said glowing with profound satisfaction. "Now for the pies!" When the pies had been shovelled into the oven Tom stood at the trestle sharpening a knife on a butcher's steel. He was reeling with excitement, pride and the level of alcohol circulating in his blood.

"'Ot bread!" he called, "Bread, butter, jam an' onion sauce. Come an' git it! Pigs be an hour yet!"

The Major's men were not used to this sort of fare. They lost interest in the subjects of debate. Hairy arms and gnarled hands, some with fingers missing, emerged, grabbing slices, getting spatulas of butter, spooning blobs of jam and sauce.

Only bush sounds could be heard. Whip birds cracked in the high trees, cat birds meeowed, dollar birds cackled as they flew about.

Tom's chooks stalked about clucking in satisfaction or squawked in outrage as they were pushed off the trestle.

"Excuse me," the Major asked of Hayward, "haven't tasted bread in years. Best I enjoy a slice before it's all gone!" He returned with a slice of the heavy bread with tamarind jam.

"Capital!" he said. "Not saying anything against your colonial damper you understand, but my! It's good to taste real bread for a change! And with butter too. Is this Tamarind I am tasting? Familiar with tamarind from India, you know."

'That so?" said Hayward. "Yeah, Tom gets it from the forest. There's not much he doesn't know about native tucker."

"Do you rent him out to approved clients occasionally?"

"I'd 'ave to put the kibosh on that idea Major." Hayward said, laughing.

Things seemed to going tops he thought. A bloke could almost get to like this stuck-up cove.

The Major too, thought he was settling in well.

"Damned fine camp you have here Hay, what?"

"Got a good team." he replied modestly. "Lost two of 'em Major."

"Lost two of them? What do you mean?"

"I brought blacks from Sorrel's run down on the Yarrandabbie. Top-hole fellas. Been with us f'r years. Murdered out on the flats. 'Appened a few weeks back."

Blacks as 'top-hole fellows?

"I'm sorry to hear of it. But there's bound to be trouble with savages. I've given them a sharp warning. They leave us well alone."

"You mightn't 'ave 'eard the last of that either, Major. Bert tells me you keep a man on guard. That's good if you wanted to vet tramps. Nothing in this country is anything like anything you ever knowed. Look – it's Christmas an' I don't wanna get ya goat but I gotta tell ya - if the blacks wanna wage war on us it'll 'appen so slow ya won't know about it till it hits. I know 'em. They ain't so stupid as we think. Ya gotta go cautious an' leave off the raids. Now I'll shut me gob. Another beer?"

The Major considered these words in stony silence as his ire rose. He didn't come here to be preached to by a young colonial illiterate.

"I appreciate your concern," he lied. "However, young fella, I'm no new chum to natives. Learnt how to handle natives in India, you know."

A thinner mug would have crumpled in Hayward's hand.

The very idea of savages waging war was ridiculous. War required discipline, intelligence, planning and as he knew well, central and local command under a system of hierarchical authority. War? Ridiculous! The young lad was an ignorant fool, but a likable one in spite of his bad temper and manners. As a seasoned, world-traveled and educated man of superior rank he should not be too hard on the poor fellow.

"But thank you, young man." Hayward tried to hide the tightness of his jaw, "And thank you for this splendid – what did you call it? Shindig? We're the only civilized community in the wilderness. You've done a sterling job. It's good we are sharing Christmas dinner, what?"

When Ben Morgan strolled up, Hayward was glad to get away.

"G'day Ben. 'Old on a tick – gotta go water the horse."

"Come an' git it!" Tom bellowed, banging a spoon against a plate. He and the blacks had quartered and sliced the pigs and wrapped the remainder in canvas. (Tom kept the trotters and ears for pickling.) Corncobs and potatoes lay in steaming paper bark. A camp oven full of wild greens flavored with bush spices sat on the trestle with a huge ladle sticking out of it. It was a sight like some of the men had never seen. It was talked about and dreamed about years later.

The general hubbub died down as the men began to eat, standing about in groups, sitting on logs in rows, squatting or perched on stumps.

ॐ

The two new blacks were kept busy tending the fire under the pies. They were glad they had come with the bullocky. This was a good life compared to life in the gully at the settlement. They wore hand-me-downs and had three meals a day, tobacco and rum some nights. They learnt what they had to be taught remarkably quickly, ignoring as best they could the imponderable mysteries of their situation. Having an old hand such as Turnip to guide them eased the strain.

Here, in the camp of the boss man, a little of that old feeling of belonging was coming to them again. They were feeling that they were one of a close-knit group. It was far distant from knowing that you were one of a family whose antecedents went back to the beginnings of time but this was what kept them striving, by work, to be a part of this new life they could not understand. Their huge white smiles were becoming more frequent now. Their powers of mimicry and observation, unbeknown to them, were their real teachers.

The Major ignored them. He disapproved of the way Hayward and his men treated them as one of themselves, though they were still at work. The Major knew the best way to treat natives. Arms length and a tight hand.

"Eh there! Billy and Jacky, better knock off a spell. Grab some tucker before all these white bastards polish it off." Tom called.

The Major winced. White bastards! What, eat with them? This was a dangerous business. He should talk to the young fellow about this – as if it were possible to teach these damn colonials the right way to do anything.

But Turnip, Quartpot, Billy and Jacky knew their place in the white man's camp. They sat together on a log by the edge of the camp with a tin plate on their knees eating python with their fingers. The Major could not know that they were not subservient in this. They were simply giving to the white man the same respect they would have given the elders in their tribal days.

The men didn't take much notice. Replete at least for a while, they sat about mingling now, smoking pipes, a few chewing tobacco, still fewer smoking cigars.

The Major took a leather cigar case from his pocket and lit one of the last of his cheroots. He picked a stick up from the pit fire to light it with. He sat on a stump there quietly enjoying the bite of tobacco and the aroma of the smoke. The meal was the best he had eaten since leaving Sydney years ago. There was more to come. He was very content.

Ben came over and sat by him, haunches on heels.

"Major," he said, "This mob have sent four dray loads of cedar back to the mill."

"Egad! You don't say?"

"The Welsh bloke told me there is as many up river felled and ready to be canted into the river."

The Major thought a while.

"Ben," he said slowly. "these are Sorrel's men. They have their home at the Yarrandabbie. They've nothing to do here but work the timber. They have four niggers to do a lot of work about the place. This holding is to be my home Ben. We've cleared ten acres and sown crops. We have dug a sawpit and dressed logs and built a fine house. Later next year Mrs. Dallhousie and Emma will join us. When these chaps are still living like niggers we will have a fine farm. The cedar will still be there for us to fell won't it? Before the years out this team will have taken the best from this strip and gone home. We're bringing civilization here Ben."

"Yeh, well you tell 'em that boss, We're gittin' a ribbin' from these bastards. That cocky little bald coot asked me how long it took to polish your leathers. Any other time I'd a biffed 'im one."

The Major smiled in appreciation.

"We'll just have to show them a thing or two, eh Ben?"

He knew himself to be a man's man. A leader. A man of action. To him, all things feminine were of another world. Women didn't seem to be part of the real world.

This day reminded him of the old days. All these tough men about. Not a woman in a weeks march. Smoking nonchalantly he strolled to the dray and buckled on the one constant joy of his life – his five-shot Colt-Paterson revolver. Ben watched, still squatting on his heels.

Baldy was telling Murdy how he had a head of hair like a bear when he was born but worried it all off by the time he was two. Duncan was getting redder arguing with Owen about the Gaelic. They had recently come just short of blows about the origin of the bagpipes.

Cliff and Oscar were discussing the possibility of a certain part of a Chinese woman's anatomy being on the horizontal. They decided to ask Walt, who had been on the Shanghai run. But he thought it best not to destroy an old myth with the mundane truth.

Tom was bragging about his friend Bill King, famous as the Flying Pieman.

"I wuz boozin' in the Brickfield Hill pub takin' bets against 'im carrying a goat from the pub t' Parramatta in under ten hours. Well, I'm 'ere t' tell ya 'e did it in seven. I knowed as it were me wot did the weighin. That bloody goat came in at seven stone one pound an' four ounces – fair dinkum!"

The Major's top dog was at odds with Bain Walsh about the finer points of saw sharpening. Bert and Hayward were in deep conversation about the virtues of the American axe, spruce handles and linseed oil. The others were bragging about teams who felled the most timber in a day, blokes who had shot the most duck, drank the most beer, sheared the most sheep, or single-handed sowers who could out-sow double handed sowers. How many super feet Fred Hole once sawed, rare escapes from injury or death, the Major's skill with firearms and how he ran his camp like a military establishment, all inspired by the bushman's innate bravado, strength and endurance and their love of excesses and prowess.

It all came to a sudden stop when the Major fired his pistol in the air. Turnip froze, standing stock still on his way to the river with a pile of dishes. The other three blacks made for the timber.

"Now I have your attention," the Major said.

About five yards away a cicada was singing on the trunk of a gum.

"Keep an eye on that insect," he said, turning his body sideways, his right arm extended from the shoulder, his left hand under the elbow to support the heavy weapon. Another loud report and there was a neat hole where the cicada used to be. The men roared approval. In another six seconds other holes appeared around it.

The Major's men, redeemed, beamed at each other. The Major thrilled. He wondered if he could do it again. He was in his element when Hay's men crowded around to inspect the revolver.

The spirit of competition roused, a shoot was proposed. Hayward brought out the old Baker muskets that had served time in the Peninsular War.

"Right oh, who's the fastest shot?"

Four men tried to best each other at loading and firing the muzzle-loaders with fair accuracy at a blaze on a tree. Colin Webster, ex New South Wales Corps, won that one with two shots a minute and four hits. There were foot races, hop, step and a jump competitions, games of two-up, wrestling matches and marbles. Turnip, Billy and Jacky were pitted against each other in a tree-climb. Turnip won and was rewarded with the tomahawk he used and a packet of Nigger Twist.

When the time came for a mug of tea and the pies it was getting dark.

A happy band of tired men sat around the fire reminiscing about the day's events while the remaining food was eaten cold. The blacks, who had enjoyed the day as much as any, seeing it as the white man's sort of corroboree, sat on their log watching with interest, wondering at these strange people who had come and taken their life away. Old Tom lay in an alcoholic stupor next to his brandy bottle down in the cellar. Ben Morgan, who had competed in almost every event, was asleep in the wagon. Heads began to nod. Less and less was said.

The Major felt that all was right with the world. He had enjoyed a day of manly sport in which his men had shown their metal.

"A grand day, Redpath. Our sincere thanks. A fine gesture on your part too, dear boy. But my men are tuckered out. Best rouse them and get on back, what? By the way...tell old Tom the snake was delicious!"

Hay laughed. The Major gave Murdy who was nodding off on the next stump, a nudge with his boot. "I say there sailor, go find Ben. Tell him to rouse some men to unyard the bullocks and get hitched up."

Tired and calm the men grouped about the wagon. Hayward's men gathered around. The two groups were separated again. The Major, too tired to ride, hitched the stallion to the wagon and climbed into it and sat on the plank next to Ben. Ben flicked his whip on the lead bullock. "Walk!" he yelled. The wagon with its cargo of happy men moved slowly.

The men called softly; so long Bain...toodelloo Murdy...hooray Owen...bye Bert... be seein' ya...

The wagon lumbered off into the dappled night.

Ben and the Major kept watch as the men dozed. With no mishap they forded the river and followed the track in good light up to the homestead.

Ben looked at the Major to see if he was awake. He was, though he was dreaming of Thora and Emma and the fine, more dignified Christmases they would have in the years to come.

"Smell smoke." Ben said.

"Eh? What? Smoke eh." The Major said dreamily.

They rolled into the home yard. No dog barked. The men dozed on. Ben and the Major sat upright now, alert. Eyes wide open, staring.

Smoke rose grey and slow from the remains of the house, the barracks, and even the humpies. The wagons were smouldering. The milch cows, dogs and horses were gone. Broken boxes, opened tins and stores were scattered about. Iolo Morganwg late of Clwtpatrwn in Aberystwyth, six months in the colony, lay dead, his head smashed with a nulla-nulla.

A ghostly silence hung over the clearing where the Major's future used to be.

GOING HOME

Bellingen Valley 1828 - 1840

This was a valley of plenty. Many trees gave the families fruit; there were edible plants aplenty and stands of palms for palm core and for weaving. There were berries and tubers and roots. The river mouth, lagoons and billabongs were rich in fish, turtles, ducks and sea birds; the beaches with pippies and shellfish, the mangroves with oysters, mud crabs and worms. Snakes, goannas and possums were aplenty. In the clearings the Kumbaingeri had made, many wallabies, kangaroos, bettongs, potoroos, pademelons and bandicoots came to feed.

To this favorite place the tribe came from as far north as Land Finger and as far south as Sea Bowl and from the high country, to trade, see the future, marry, gossip, sing, corroboree, feast, and to learn new songs.

❧

Mountain Kumbaingeri came down from the cold, bringing flints and Kurrajong seeds to trade for shells and cabbage tree and pandanas fronds, and perhaps sea turtle shell if they were fortunate.

This time there were 105 in Gnoolu's family with 25 elders in the fire council. Mountain Kumbaingeri had only 92 with 10 elders, for Luberawang the Great Spirit had taken many.

They met as usual on the grassy headland where the river found its way to the sea. The two Fathers made the ritual meeting, nulla-nulla, spears, and boomerangs dropped, advancing with the palms of the hands extended. But the first to meet were always the children. They ran to the beach to explore and swim, to tell the stories of times and places, of hunting and deeds, and wonder at the mysteries the old women knew.

❧

When Kadageri and Gnoolu squatted it was the sign for everyone to mingle.

Then there was much chatter and inspection of each other and admiration expressed for shell necklaces, woven baskets, and dilly bags. There was news of births, deaths, marriages, fights and squabbles. Everybody had a marvelous time. It was the season the small groups looked forward to as they wandered.

Singers started up amongst the families, singing the news and the doings, telling preposterous stories, lampooning others, taking ordinary events and singing them into marvelous myths. The victims of ribald stories rolled on the ground laughing along with everybody else.

Then they quieted as some sung of Luberawang, the dreaming of the earth and the waking in the upper land. Groups gathered about the singers, rocking back and forth as they squatted, sometimes shouting a word or meaningless sound when they saw without eyes.

They sang:

> *Red are we; red as the glowing coals in the fire,*
> *Like the glowing coals are we red with ochre,*
> *Ochre from the cliff, the cliff by the shore.*
> *Red is the fire in the sun,*
> *Glowing red swelling, longing to be home*
> *In the night.*

He goes down into the earth,
He enters the earth,
Becomes the redness of ochre.
Red are we, red as the sun entering earth,
Red as the ochre in the cliffs by the shore.

They sang together their favorite song – of how every single thing on earth was from a star in the night sky and that all people were children of the sun and that the moon was their mother who ruled over all the changes in their lives. When the clapping of hands and the clicking of boomerangs and the beat of rhythm sticks slowed to silence they sat transfixed, motionless as in a dreamless sleep.

❧

As darkness came, fires were built up from the fire-sticks. Each family, including cousins, elders and those of other families who had become blood-bonded, sat about their fires. The dark was scored with the trail of fire-sticks as the young people moved from one camp to another, calling their name as they approached.

The elders watched the young ones, noting their stature and bearing. Gnoolu had sung after a dreaming that new blood was needed in the body of the family. There was much laughter and clapping of boomerangs and yam sticks, chanting and crooning of stories. So the night flowed on. By the time Kurrawong-eye rose over the horizon most were asleep, hip holes dug and backs to the fires. The dawn breeze sang softly in the casuarinas. The sound of the surf was no more than a hush. The fires crackled. The Kumbaingeri snored serenely in the peace of deep sleep.

❧

As the days passed, families arrived until every Kumbaingeri had gathered there – except of course, the strange ones who walked alone. Since the beginnings of memory it was at this corroboree that the Big Dreaming came to the best dreamer and the best dreamer by far was Gnoolu. Gnoolu had dreamed many dreams for he was so old that there was not one alive who could remember his birthing. Gnoolu's word was law amongst the Kumbaingeri. Even other tribes knew his fame so they often sent messengers to ask him to dream solutions.

ﾞ

So it was that when all the ceremonies were over and the corroboree was drawing to a close, Gnoolu ate no food. Then he paddled up-river to his special place, built two fires and sat between them to sweat the past out. Then he chanted himself into the upper land where the tribal ancestors dwelt.

The tribe waited his return anxiously. Food was dwindling, but it was not wise to leave until the content of Gnoolu's dreaming was revealed, yet that could not be done until Arunga, his woman, had heard of it for though Gnoolu saw the dream and sang the song, only the wisest of the women knew how to listen to it.

Late on the third day Gnoolu returned, tired and dispirited. With Arunga he went to the beach so they could be alone.

I do not like the taste of this talking or the sound of this song, he told her. I fear it. My spirit has sunk because of this dreaming and that is not as it should be. Hear it now and tell me of its meaning when I wake.

After singing the song softly into Arunga's ear, Gnoolu went to their fire and slept.

The Great Spirit was just lighting the earth when Arunga came into their camp. Gnoolu was sleeping restlessly, kicking and blinking like a dingo pup does when it sleeps by the fire, but is thin and unwell, full of worms.

Arunga had lost the life spirit from her eyes. She felt as she did the day she gave birth to a dead child. She was not able to accept this new knowledge either.

She picked a stone up and beat it against her forehead because it was good to feel an easy pain.

The other women looked on in silence. She took a flint knife from far beyond the mountains and scored herself from her birth cave to her throat. She squatted and looked about her as if called from many places and hung her head between her knees and rocked slowly back and forth. The other women watched in silence that she might suffer in dignity though they too, knew consternation. They watched as she went to the river and rubbed clay into the wound and the bruise on her forehead then walked slowly into the forest and was gone.

She was gone a day and a night. The women knew her sorrow so not one said her name or spoke of her going or wounding herself because that would be rude. To those who asked, where is the elder woman? They said, the Sun Spirit has called her away.

They had gathered a food offering for Gnoolu of well-soaked cycad nuts and pippies and mud oysters in a turtle shell bowl with the blood of a wallaby and the seeds of water lilies. Special foods, but Gnoolu did not eat. He wondered what the song meant and why Arunga was gone a day and a night.

The fire council sat around her when she returned, waiting for her to speak. They saw that she was greatly changed. It was an uneasy feeling to sit and wait while she looked tenderly at each one. Then she rose and went around the sacred circle touching each chin and clucking her tongue slowly. Some wiped their eyes for this was the gesture of love, rarely given.

Sitting, she said, Elder women, a great change is coming. Before your daughter's children have grown to fullness, the Kumbaingeri will be no more. The Great Spirit wants us back.

There followed great wailing and a beating of breasts and many questions. Most would not believe but knew that ever since they could remember, everything Gnoolu and Arunga had sung came to pass.

Do we not know that this life in the low world is as a dreaming? Arunga said, reassuring them, after our passing we will be Kumbaingeris in the warm heart of the sun and corroboree and sing great songs there as we do here. We will be going home.

When, how, why, how will we tell the time is near? The elders asked.

Strange others are coming with which we can make no families or go walkabout. The earth is sad because she will weep for us when we are no more and will be lonely. The strange ones will be separated far from home while we will all be together. Before this comes about there will be much suffering. Signs will be sent. I have put all this onto a big message stick. It is hidden with the other sacred things to be read by the Dreamer in his time. I will tell Gnoolu these things and he will tell the men elders and we will keep this secret and speak of it no more.

❧

The time of parting had come. Who was going where and with whom? New alliances needed support and old enemies required snubbing, so there was much shouting and bickering; sometimes confusion and uproar, pleasing everybody. They parted with many gesticulations, recriminations, mild and humorous abuse or a shaking of spears, with much chin touching and tongue clicking. They did not like to see a great corroboree go out like an unattended fire. They walked their ways glad at heart – except those who knew of Gnoolu's dreaming.

ॐ

The days went by. Many forgot the time when Arunga behaved so strangely. The elders kept their secret and passed on the knowledge of the message stick in the sacred place.

Seasons spun their eternal round. The last of the elders of Arunga's time died when she became a burden to the family, so she went by cutting her wrists at the blood rivers and going happily to the upper land as the others sung her away.

Other songs were sung and there were wonders that kept them happy and wondering and arguing far into the night. Some said they had seen strange things on the sea like birds with huge white wings swimming like gulls but longer than trees. There were rumors of animals like nothing ever seen before or even imagined. Huge beasts with six legs that became like men with two legs sometimes and like men animals with four legs and one huge head sometimes. But others nodded sagely saying this is from too much chewing of kaditcha leaves so the eyes make pictures.

ॐ

For two days a violent storm battered the coast. Its coming was sung so the families wove buroolas from pandanas leaves that covered their heads and backs, built gunyas and cooked goannas and snakes, collected lilly-pillies and figs and huddled in the gunyas keeping the fire-sticks alight.

When the storms passed, a strange thing was found on the beach. Its tracks like no tracks ever seen before, told the people that it had come out of the sea. Smoke was sent up telling others to come, so by the time the thing moved there were many standing looking and arguing about what it might be.

Wolumbi argued that if it was a sea creature it was a strange one indeed for it had no fins. Nimmiti wondered about its heavy coverings, or was it another skin?

Domagi said it was a covering for you could see white skin sticking out. Perhaps it was a creature from the upper lands, washed down by the storm.

Who ever heard of white skin Nimmiti said.

But it has hands, arms and legs like us. It does not have wings Botunga objected.

Such a thing could not be imagined if it had not first been seen said Gumuloo. It brings bad omens. We should kill it and throw it back.

Then Wolumbi said that perhaps it was a good omen and it may be from the upper lands and could do great talking and powerful dreaming and knew marvelous songs. Killing it would bring down wrath.

The people seeing this creature were half frightened and half amused and a lot awed so that when it groaned and coughed water they jumped back startled.

The warrior Woolunguluk fitted his spear into his woomera. He waited. Others stood by with nulla-nullas ready.

Coming into the group, the elder said, Do not hurt it! it is a sun creature like us.

Perhaps that is why it is such an unnatural colour.

The creature sat up looking startled. It was easy to see its fear. It made strange sounds that made the people look at each other in wonder. A young one, making pretence of courage, went to touch the creature but when the creature stood up, he jumped back in fright. The strange one tottered and collapsed. It made an angry noise.

Kulug, the brightest and most mischievous of youths, jumped forward and grabbed the creature by the foot. He screamed in surprise as its covering came away. Gumuloo grabbed the other one.

It was a more amazing thing than the creature itself. Everybody rushed upon them to see these things, hold them, or try to put them on. Everyone marveled at the bright things on top but they could not be pulled off. When Nimmiti got them she tried to put them on and her feet went in so they could not be seen.

Bollaroo, the big father, said this is a creature the same as us. It makes strange sounds that might be talk. And only people talk and walk and have feet. But I do not know why it is covered in this bright bark or why it has skin such a colour. The old rumors from Gnuloo's time said such weird things would come about in the strange times that were to come.

He stopped speaking as the creature staggered to its feet again. The creature seemed to take heart. He pointed to his chest and said Lieutenant Browning over and over. Bright Woolunguluk practiced under his breath and then tried to make the same sounds but the first one would not come out. The creature smiled, nodding and said it again. Woolunguluk pointed to his heart and said Woolunguluk many times and waited. They were all breathless with excitement as they waited. They gasped and danced about laughing when the creature pointed to Woolunguluk and said his name.

Everybody had to have their name said by the stranger, so there was such gibberish of sounds that it confused the creature and it made signs they could understand. Before half of them had had their name said the creature wavered and sat down, pointing to its mouth and making a sound. Food! Kulug echoed.

Some of the women who had come running had coolums with fruits, berries, yams and roots in them, so they put them in front of the creature and it ate them all. It signed for water so they signed back for it to follow them to the creek. It amazed them to see the creature could not walk properly upon the stones without its foot coverings. Botunga said it proved that this creature was from the upper lands where everything is as smoke and mist.

It did not belong to the earth he said, and his argument carried much weight.

After it had water it was important to know what it was. It did not have milk breasts. Bollaroo made the creature take off its coverings to see if it was a man or a woman. This made the creature angry, then ashamed. This is a very strange creature indeed said Bollaroo. The coverings were given back because no one wanted them after they had been played with. Botunga's insistence was ignored for creatures from the upper lands do not need childmakers and such coverings. Bollaroo called the creature Weri Boroo meaning bright bark. Nimmiti said she thought it was her husband come back from the ancestor's lands. She gave him back his foot coverings and began to look after him. The others smiled though some thought it might be so. Nimmiti built a gunya for him and kept him warm at night with her possum rug and her body. One night he came into her birth place so she made a song about it, making more mysteries. She sang that Weri Boroo was not her husband returned from the upper lands, nor could he be from the upper lands or from the earth for he coupled like the birds! He even planted his seed before the ground was wet! The families stayed up all night arguing about this strange person no one could understand. Bollaroo remembered old rumors about Gnuloo's dreaming. He said he would go to the sacred place and read the mysteries stored there. He remembered the rumor about the things no one could understand that would come as a sign that something of great importance was about to happen. Singers took the story so it was sung from family to family.

&

Even then, their carefree life was coming to an end. Gossip about it poisoned their spirits and disturbed their sleep. A new thing had come amongst them along with the strange being. It was never spoken but haunted them like the unseen ghost of a dead enemy.

One morning Nimmiti woke to find Weri Boroo gone and was grateful. No one looked for him. They tried hard to forget.

But stories came with traders from far to the south that were much more puzzling. Things beyond understanding and about which they could know nothing, fretted the memory and vexed the spirit so much that a child was once slapped in anger.

At night they sat about their fires talking of nothing but the stories and if they were true. They spoke of those who said they had been with these strange white spirit people though no one actually knew anybody who had done so. There were stories of such strangeness that many would not believe no matter what they heard – or who told them. It was said that some of the white people changed their coverings many times in a day. Gumulu said he could not see why anyone would want to be covered head to toe at all so why get in and out of different coverings unless it was a madness? The rumors said that many stayed camped together in the one place all the time and lived in big gunyas larger than the biggest cave. They floated wherever they wanted to go over the water in the birds with big wings. They all had a lot of the same tools made from strange stones and though everybody had their own separate things they fought about them often. This the Kumbaingeri could not find a reason for. Woolunguluk said it was not hard to see these strange ones were quite mad. This made everybody feel better because it was known that people so strange as to be mad were dreaming with the gods.

But when they heard that they could make fire with a wave of the hand and had spears that could kill without leaving the woomera, and that they had frightful beasts that pulled houses that moved with them inside so they did not have to walk, the people became angry. They knew that these things were impossible.

Wolumbi shook his spears and said what are these white ones doing in our land? Why have they come to make our thoughts troubled and disturb our sleep with bad dreams? Let us gather with the other tribes and go and throw them out!

Bollaroo was at that fire. He had returned from reading the messages on Arunga's message stick.

There is no need to go, Bollaroo said. It will not be long before they are here. I will not gather the warriors for it is not the wish of Gnoolu and the ancestors that we fight battles with the white skinned people. Oldest father in the fire council, noble Bollaroo said no more. True to the wisdom of Gnoolu and Arunga he kept the secret but it was too much to bear, this knowledge that there would come a day when the tribes would go walkabout or corroboree no more. They had done this since the beginning of time in their ancient land. He wondered what they had done to offend Luberawang. They had been true to the totems and had kept the lore. How could such a thing be? The sadness festered in him like an open wound, worse because it could not be shared.

He withered like a leaf on a broken twig, and died.

The news spread from family to family and by the time the favorite time came again the people were not the same. There had been many councils held about it and much argument was brought to the corroboree. Wolumbi was for war but the fire council forbade it seeing that Bollaroo had read the stick. Nevertheless, Wolumbi gathered many young warriors and went to the southlands to turn the white skins back. They were never seen again. There was great wailing in the camps. The elder men and women in the fire circles were silent with grief that the young no longer heeded the advice of the elders. Families were sundered, there were many spearings. The families looked at each other with distrust and suspicion. The people could not understand why the elders did not laugh any more. When they all died within a year of each other the people grew afraid.

The young men who once thought of the mysteries and wanted nothing better than to be an elder sitting in the sacred circle about the fire no longer thought so. Many left their family and totem, nor did they sing the sacred chant when they killed. At night around the fires, they did not sing the songs of the old ones but went apart. Adventurous ones went off to watch the marvels spoken of and were not seen again.

That year sounds were heard in the valley of the big river, such as were never heard before. Sounds like the crack of thunder, the ringing of stone on stone and the crash of falling trees. Sorrel's men had pushed up from the Yarrandabbie to plunder the rainforest of its cedar.

Hayward Redpath and his team had started felling the cedar in the valley of the Kumbaingeri. It was a marvelous opportunity. It meant that all the riches life could offer, independence and wealth would be theirs, but deep in the ancient people of the rivers was a knowing so poignant that it had no words. They knew with a dark knowing that going home meant that their life was to end.

ARCHIE AND BONNEY

Port Macquarrie- Bellinger River - 1840

Archie had a right to complain about the star he had been born under.

His father could have been any one of the soldiers in the British garrison in Dublin. He was born in the slums in the establishment where his mother rented a room as needs be at threepence a time. He pimped for his mother until syphilis got the better of her. At eight he followed the horse fairs and markets, stealing, picking pockets, begging, or helping a flimflam man turn a trick.

At twenty Archie stole a steak and kidney pie with which to ease the gnawing pain in his stomach. When the owner of the pie attempted to regain possession, Archie committed an assault.

These errors earned him fourteen years transportation to the penal colony at Port Jackson. By the time he got there his back bore stripes from the cat o' nine tails.

In spite of all this Archie had a sense of humour and a playful attitude to being alive, made possible by having no scruples, no morals and a habit of always taking the way of least resistance. Archie was not one for the up-hill struggle.

The colony was so desperate for workers that after a few hellish years he was given a ticket-of-leave and sent to work for the Macarthurs at Cowpastures. He washed wool; he learned to shear and ride and handle a brace of horses behind a plow. He spent dangerous lonely weeks in bark huts at the edge of wilderness as a shepherd. He became strong and self-reliant but he was still a rascal. Because he was reasonably well fed and clothed and almost free, and not too tempted, he stayed on after he served his time. But one day, with plenty of food inside and a lot in a bundle, jingling holey dollars in his pocket he set out for Sydney Town.

Before the month was gone his life became complicated, so much so that he began to fear it might be brought to an unpleasant sort of halt.

Archie stowed away on a coastal schooner, hid in the pinnace with a loaf of bread and a bottle of water and sailed north.

When the bread ran out he attempted to sneak into the galley, was discovered, given a thrashing and put to work twenty hours out of twenty-four. Long hours of hard work had become the norm for Archie.

The ship anchored at a settlement that had no official name. The few locals called it 'the anchorage.' By this time Archie had charmed most of the crew. He found it easy to steal some food, a knife, blanket and a jacket and singing a prison ditty, jumped ship while they were too drunk to notice. By dawn he was miles south, sitting in the bush getting breakfast.

The next day he climbed a tree on the edge of the settlement to spy on the harbour. The schooner had gone, so Archie went to savor the delights of the town. Within two hours he had it well conned. Where the vegetable patches were, troopers barracks, pubs, doss houses, shanties (good places for scrounging or stealing tucker) stables and other good places to kip down out of wind and rain.

Then it was down to business. That night outside the pub, he tempted a sodden wayfarer with a tale of his desirable sister who had an inordinate weakness for nimble little Irish lads spare of limb and tight of arse. This description fitted O'Flynn, tempting him beyond his capacity to resist.

A few more descriptions of his sister's proclivities and O'Flynn was ready to follow Archie wherever he might lead.

So it was that O'Flynn was relieved of the money his boss had given him for the purchase of tools and provisions and Archie had come into possession of twenty-four pounds eleven shillings and sixpence, a greatcoat, and a hip flask with a mouthful or two of brandy in it.

Archie had also come into possession of O'Flynn's knowledge of the big money to be made up north, so Archie determined to enjoy the best of the worst ladies in town, have three big meals a day, drink his share, smoke as much as he pleased, roll a few more tricks and go investigate the cedar-getting business. He was going to try to appear to be respectable, as long as it wasn't too much trouble.

Hard work for a big reward would be easy for Archie, after years of hard work on the Western Road over the mountains with nothing but a leaky tent and scant food. There was only one thing that didn't interest him about his new plans, and that was doing it alone.

One of the best of the ladies he enjoyed was Matilda Sarah Bonnington. Though he admired the elegance of her name as well as her ample form, Archie preferred to call her Bonney. And bonny she was. In a coarse, tough, though honest sort of way.

Bonney was not too tall and not too short. She was not too stout and not too thin, she was not too fair and not too plain. But the thing Archie really liked about Bonney was that she was not too fussy.

Bonney's mother was a black. Her father was one of the soldiers with Oxley's expedition that came through in the twenties, so they had a lot in common. She could pass for a Spaniard or Italian until she said something.

She was known in the town as the half-caste whore, which was only partially true because she had a job as scullion in the pub. In his first step to what he judged as respectability, Bonney got him a job there as ostler, and many a night they enjoyed in the hayloft.

By combining honest and dishonest livelihoods and pooling the profits, Bonney and Archie soon had a tidy sum in their kitty. Christmas festivities at the pub gave them a good chance to add to their swag and by late December they were ready to go.

On the twenty-ninth at six o'clock in the morning they paid a boatman to row them over the harbour to the southern end of the beach that stretched in a great curve to the horizon.

They joked and chattered with the boatman as they unloaded their things. Archie offered to toss him double or nothing when it came to pay up but the boatman was no fool.

They both wore greatcoats, the pockets full of seeds: goosefoot, arrowroot, corn, turnip, cauliflower, oats and barley. They carried two loaves of bread and some apples, tinderboxes, water bottles and utensils. From a rope about his waist Archie carried a billycan, pot and fry pan. Slung across his back, a swag of two rolled blankets with tea, sugar and flour in calico bags rolled inside. Roped to the swag were an axe and a crosscut saw. Around his neck he carried a bag with a roll of corned beef, pipe and tobacco, three boxes of cartridges and some spuds. In the crook of an arm he carried his prize possession – a double barrelled shotgun, recently stolen.

On her back Bonney carried a wicker basket with two hens and a rooster in it from Mrs. Wilson's chook run.

It was a fine clear morning to begin an adventure. A light breeze blew off the breakers, cicadas sung lustily in the scrub over the sand hills. Gulls screamed and wheeled at them as they struggled down to the wet, firmer sand.

"Ow'll we know wen we gits there?" Bonney wanted to know.

"We gotta keep a look out f'r a tidy little sort of mountain goin' up to a point close to the coast an just on a bit two rivers come together at a beach an' the valley wid the best cedar are, runs west up the north arm. Should be easy as fallin' off of a log."

For the first few minutes they talked as they walked. Soon there was little breath left to talk. They trudged on, their eyes fixed on the grey blur of sand before their feet.

When the sun rose to mid-heaven they went over the sand hills into the scrub. They collapsed as soon as their burdens were off and were asleep within minutes.

When they woke they boiled the billy and ate some bread and a round of corned beef.

Groaning, they loaded up, made down to the firm sand and trudged on.

By the end of the day Bonney was close to collapse from heat and exhaustion. The greyness swam before her eyes, the pounding of the surf blurred her thinking, drummed into her brain so she could not feel her pain.

She staggered as she walked, the toes of her laced-up boots leaving scoops out of the wet sand. Long before, she had put the chin ribbon of her bonnet into her mouth. Her teeth bit tightly upon it.

"Must 'ave a break," Archie muttered, heading towards the scrub. The deep dry sand was too much for them, so they collapsed there in a haze of exhaustion.

After a rest they left most of their clobber there and went into the scrub to make a fire and bed down for the night. They were so tired that it was difficult to stay awake to eat the roasted spuds. By seven o'clock they lay on their coats with arms wrapped about each other snoring.

When they woke their legs were so stiff it was difficult to stand. Their backs ached.

"The Devil take it!" Archie complained from between clenched teeth. "We're all seized up stiff as a poker. Oh well lass, take heart - it'll pass off. There's nought for us but t' keep at it."

"I'm more the fool f'r listenin' to your madcap plans Archibald Conners. Another day as the last jist gawn an' you'll be 'avin a dead body on ya hans I swear. There's no prudery in me black arf so it's off with these bloody boots Archie. I'm gettin' rid of this dress an' petticoats an' all. I'll be down t' me bloomers t'day Mr. Conners!"

"Come on then, me Bonney, lets down t' the beach an' git loaded up. It's only another few days o' trudgin' an' the weather's fair."

He was wrong. A few days of trudging brought them to a wide river meandering through rich alluvial plains and the forest was so dense they could not penetrate it to find a ford further up. Archie stood and scratched his head.

"Stone the bloody crows," he said, "wots to do now?"

"Wot we do now is make a boat and float across," Bonney replied.

"Strewth! We gotta do that every time we comes to a bloomin' river? Ow many we gotta get over Gawd knows."

"No sweat. Me mum showed me ow t' make one easy see. We strips a few ov' them paper bark trees an piles it up in a heap, ties it together a bit with vines and she floats good as gold. We piles our stuff on an swims 'er over"

They had little idea what lay at the end of their journey nor did they give it any thought. Putting one foot down after the other took all their attention. They didn't realise that they were not so much going towards anything, as they were going *away* from something. They knew that they were not so much going from one place to another but one time to another. They had left the past. They were walking toward the future.

A week later they sat in silent exhaustion in front of the fire, thinking. Archie was worried that the slogging was too much for Bonney.

"'Ow yer goin,' love?" he asked putting an arm over her shoulder and drawing her to him.

She took a long time to reply.

"Oh Archie I'm all done in. I had such an easy life at the 'arbour. Now look at me!" And she wept against his chest until he could feel the tears soak through to his flesh.

"Jeezus love. I know, I know. You've got the guts for it so we'll git there an' do well, you see! But I've been thinkin. Wots the bloody hurry aye? Let's take our time an' take it easy. We don't 'ave t' be the first there do we?"

"Mum always said I was a right little whinger." She kissed the stubble on his cheek. Archie wept too, wiping his eyes on his sleeve.

They sat weeping, hugging and rocking each other until sleep overtook them.

So they took their time, swimming in the rivers or taking a dip in the ocean and not rationing the food they brought. They caught fish and shot a kangaroo and Bonney went off to find native tucker. It was the closest thing to a holiday they had ever known.

Weeks later they were sauntering along chatting when Archie said, "Look Bonney, that must be the little mountain that silly little bastard told me about. Jeesus Bonney! I reckon we're there. Well! 'Ow about that then! Give us a kiss!"

They shook the burdens off, threw the overcoats on the ground and lay near naked upon them hugging and kissing. Inevitably Archie got ideas.

"Orl right, Archibald Conners. Put that thing away. We aren't 'ome yet!" Bonney protested.

"Stone the bloody crows, Bonney! That's wot you bloody well said last bloody time!"

Imploring didn't work with Bonney.

Archie stood, got into the coat and swag and stomped off through the bush.

"Ya bloody fool! Don't go stompin' off like I done yer dirt!" she yelled at him.

He waited. Bonney put the chooks on her back and the overcoat over the basket. When she had caught up with him, she put her arm through his, gave him a radiant smile and kissed his stubble.

"You bloody sheilas got me beat," said Archie.

Walking over the flats inland amongst the big paper barks and gnarled old Banksias they came to the two rivers and crossed the first one within an hour on a paper bark raft. They pushed on, lighted in spirit by knowing the trek was nearly over, and enjoying the difference of the forest of gums without much scrub. The going was easy.

They had topped a small rise amongst a stand of tall gums. The valley stretched east and west. By chance they had come upon a stretch of the river far below that worked by Sorrels' men. They could see the river curve in a huge loop. Dense rainforest filled the river flat.

"Well mate, I reckon this is as gooder place f'r us as any. Wot-ya say? Will we stake a claim?"

"My bloody oath," said Bonney. "It looks grand don't it?"

"There's a bit ov a clearin' top o' yonder rise I reckon's a good place f'r a camp."

"My Gawd Archie we're lookin' at the last few furlongs! Just think! T'morra there'll be no more trudgin'!"

"'Ow about we declares t'morra a public 'olidy."

"Too right!"

"T'morra we'll take a spell an' look 'er over."

"Then we gotta put a humpy up. An' a coop f'r the chooks. An' get some seeds in. An'..."

"'Ere! Slow down w'y dontcha? All in good time. All in good time. Day after t'morra or day afta that, 'oo cares?"

Archie could not believe that all this was his for the taking with no recriminations. He smiled a broad grin. For the first time in his life he could take something and be respected for it.

They set up camp on the rise. With her earth knowledge Bonney said, "There's a little creek down there I'll bet." She went to investigate. Not fifty yards down the rise a small creek ran over gravel on a rocky base. It was indeed an excellent place for a camp.

Next day they walked up the hill behind the rise to look down on the beauty of it all.

"I reckon there's a coupla 'undred acres down there, Mistress Bonnington" Archie joked.

''An a fine sort of bloody squire you'll be makin", Mr. Conners. Look atcha!"

Then as they stood looking, she said softly, "Archie, wot if we're countin' our chickens afore they're 'atched?"

"Gawd 'elp us! We is squatters we is. See anyone else about? House, barn, stables, yards? No bloody sir yer don't. We come an' we claimed it an' that's that. 'Course it'll 'ave t' be gazetted one day wen I gits t' some place wid a court 'ouse."

They sat on a fallen log.

"Now wot I reckon is we gits an 'umpy up first thing. You finish it up an' I'll clear a bit down near the creek an' we can git some seed in. Next thing is I find a bit o' right timber f'r makin' a plow from an' we can turn some more ground. I'll 'ave t' pull the bloody thing til we gets a bullock. Then down comes that cedar, Bonney. 'Red gold' it is they say. Now I don't rightly know 'ow we is goin' to cash it in but the point is Bonney as it's ous an worth a bloody fortune an' that's wot'll set us up fine."

"Where will we git a bullock from?"

"A bullock? How the hell would I know, woman? Any'ow we'll git a bullock an' I can do the plowin' an you can trim the logs. Let's see if we can push through t' the river."

Down on the flats they found raspberry bushes, rosella and native cherry. Native parsnips grew about the rocks and stones. About the creek dock grew and the banks were overgrown with wild spinach. By the time they got back to camp Archie carried two ducks he had shot and Bonney had an armful of native tucker. They dined well that night. When Archie got back from getting water from the creek, Bonney had the greatcoats spread out and the fire well stacked. She lay naked under a petticoat. Archie was about to clean the shotgun.

"Archie!" She called.

"Wot now?"

"Archie, where's that thing you've been pesterin' me with?"

Six months later Hayward and Bert sailed down the river in the schooner 'George Sorrel' with their first cargo of cedar. On the way up to their stash at the first rapids they had not seen any sign of Archie and Bonney. Lounging on the roof of the deckhouse they heard the ring of steel on steel as Archie drove a dog into a length of hardwood.

They saw Bonney at the water's edge having a wash. They went to the gunwale and yelled, "G'day missus! 'Ow ya goin down 'ere?"

Startled, Bonney didn't know what to say.

"'Ow long youse blokes been on this stretch?"

"About a half-year." She called back, still confused by the unexpected sight of her own kind.

"Well I'll be damned. There's a bit o' action further up." As they drew slowly around the bend Hay called, "Goin' down t' Port. Anything we can git ya?"

This woke Bonney up.

"A pick an' a mattock!" she yelled back.

Hay waved. "Rightoh! Toodelloo!"

Another two months of hard work and things were looking different at the big bend. Patches of the forest were bare. There was a track down to the river and a humpy on a hill. A vegetable garden with a brush fence grew by the creek. On the richest flat trees had been felled and trimmed.

❦

The ringing of the ship's bell brought Archie and Bonney down to the river. Bert and Hayward were rowing towards them. They leaped out onto a fallen log.

"G'day there. Got your things. 'Owed ya be? Me names Hay an' this 'ere is Bert."

"Yeh. G'day there Bert, Hay." Shaking hands.

"Yeh. The missus told me. That's 'er. Bonney, this is Bert an' Hay."

"G'day missus," they said together, fumbling a handshake.

'Well, she up an' answers ya call – out of surprise ya might say. An' you blokes been kind an' fetched them things. But, ya know, well, I mean t' say, we ain't got no money an' that's the truth of it. Not a brass farthin'."

"Aw, that's too bad, but it ain't no issue 'cos you got some red gold an' we can do a deal on that I reckon. It'll be likely it'll take a while afore some moneyed coot gits a mill goin' up 'ere an' me boss 'as a stake up river an' ownes this 'ere craft an' we can git your timber to market ay?"

"Well I'll be damned! 'Ear that me girl? Ow about a cuppa?"

"Too right. Lead the way."

As they walked up the hill Bert asked how they were going.

"Not too bad. Bit slow, jist the two ov us. I'd swap the missus 'ere f'r a bullock if there was one in the offerin'."

Bonney pulled a wry face and gave him a jab with an elbow.

It was so good to have someone else to talk to that the pair kept filling their guests up with lemon myrtle tea, grass seed cakes and tart wild fruits.

"Tell you wot." Hayward said, warming to their comradeship, "'Ow about you come to our plant up river an' earn a bit o' that stuff you're short of? Just for a spell."

"Aw Cripes, I dunno. It's leavin' the missus 'ere all on 'er Pat Malone wot gits me. Ya know..."

"Well well!" Bonney said, looking heavenward, "'Ark at 'im! As if I didn't do well enough afore I knowed you, Archie Conners!"

"Yes yes Bonney I know all about that. I don't relish leavin' ya way out in the bush weeks at a time an' no one about."

"Archie Conners, I'm a sight more home in the bloody bush than you, you daft coot. Git along with ya!"

"Pays three bob a day and keep." Hayward put in slyly.

"Good God a'mighty Bonney, did ya 'ere wot the man said! Go on with ya. Ya pullin' a man's leg."

"No it's fair dinkum. Eighteen bob a week providin' ya takes Sundy off."

"Strike a bloody light, if a man puts a week in 'e gits a guinea. Strewth! If a man put in a month 'e could git 'iself a plow an' a moke too. Well girl, wodya say, ay?"

They all looked at Bonney. She put her leg up on a log and carelessly lent an elbow on a raised knee. She waived a hand at them.

"Well go on wy dontcha. Wot ya moonin 'round 'ere for? I've enough t' keep me busy 'round 'ere wot with one thing an' another, so grab ya stuff Archie. An' wen you're rollin' in dough ya can buy me somethin' nice."

While Archie was gathering up his pipe and a few belongings Hayward asked, "Have any trouble with the blacks?"

"Blacks?" Archie said, "'Ain't seen 'ide nor 'air ov 'em."

"Got a gun?"

"Too right. Got a twelve-gauge."

"The missus know how t' use it?"

"Too right she does."

"Tell 'er to lay low if there's any blacks about an' not to be shy ov usin' the gun."

"Bin givin' trouble eh?"

"Plenty last month, mostly on the other bank though."

Archie had his things in an old sugar bag.

Looking troubled and embarrassed he made to kiss Bonney goodbye but she shied away saying "Go on with ya! Git!"

She watched them walk down the flat to the river. She watched as they rowed out to the schooner and climbed the rope ladder over the gunwale. She turned as Archie turned and waved a feeble wave. She wandered about looking forlorn.

She stood looking at the hut. It was their home. She touched the stones of the fireplace they had labored so hard to put together, and Archie's mug hanging on a stick.

She went inside to the gloom of the windowless hut, touching the table they had made with the crosscut saw he had lugged all that way.

Absent-mindedly she looked about. She looked at the shotgun leaning against the wall, the clothes on their pegs. She ran her bare toes through the possum skin rug she had made. It was their bed. She threw herself down upon it sobbing.

When Archie walked home with his spoils tied in a bundle across his back his heart pounded with excitement and trepidation. As he caught sight of the humpy through the trees tears clouded his vision. Through the misty images he saw a tall blackfellow standing on one leg, the sole of the other resting upon the inside of the thigh. One hand rested behind his back, the other held the spear he leaned on.

Terrified for Bonney, praying that it was not too late, Archie untied his tools, took the adze and crept closer. He thought he would go around the other side where the black could not see him approach, creep around the offside of the humpy and fell him with the adze. On hands and knees, he was about to move when he caught sight of a movement. It was Bonney. She came out of the hut. She walked up to the black and gave him something. The black took it, inclining his head as they do, and put it in his mouth.

Archie dropped the weapon-to-be and jumped to his feet.

"Bonney! Oh Lord, Bonney!" He yelled as he ran for the hut.

Bonney wheeled about. She saw him running and ran too. They hit each other with such force they fell mumbling their fears and joys incoherently.

When they had calmed down sufficiently to put two words together Archie said, "Bonney! The black! You alright then?"

"Oh that one? That's old Mooloolah. He's bin 'ere weeks. Just stands there lookin' about an' takin' wot food I gives 'im. The oil in 'is lamp is runnin' out."

Sometimes Bonney said the strangest things. Archie couldn't be bothered to figure them out.

The old black could not tell them he was sick at heart at their coming and what was happening to his people. He had come to this favorite place for he hoped his time to die had come. He was surprised and curious when he found the hut and watched it for days. He felt sorry for the lone woman and admired her courage. He wondered where her man was.

She found him as he lay in the timber wondering how long it would take him to die and how hungry he would get if it took too many days. He put his palms out as he lay, smiled, and closed his eyes again. He tried to die very hard but the ancestors did not come for him. He wondered if this was just another of the things to go wrong in the bad age Gnoolu had sung about.

Later, he heard her click her tongue at him. He smelt hot meat. She had brought him food. This was a strange time indeed. It was difficult to know what best to do. Then he thought he should eat the food while he waited for the ancestors. Then he felt so much better he thought maybe he wasn't able to die just now. So he went to stand not far from the hut so she wouldn't have to go so far to feed him. Then he began bringing Bonney food. She brought it back to him cooked so it tasted new and wonderful. At night as he sat about a little fire chanting, it came to him that he was meant to look after these strange ones until the ancestors came.

When Archie came up to him, he inclined his head in that depreciating way of his. He showed his palms. Archie was confused. He was close to a wild black. Bonney nudged him, shaking her head towards his hands. Cripes! There she goes again! Archie thought.

"Show 'im your bloody palms, ya oaf," she said. She spoke to the black in the dialect of the Port tribes, close enough to the Kumbaingeri tongue for the old man to understand. He nodded.

Bonney and the old black had been busy. There were rows of corn sprouting. Seed potatoes lay in the rich earth, budding. Arrowroot shoots were inches high. She had ringbarked many trees to let light down onto the ground and had felled, chopped and stacked saplings.

Archie found the right limb to make a plow from. He took the blade off a shovel and fashioned a plowshare. This he nailed to a stump off the limb. Mooloolah showed him how to make binding resin from the Kangaroo Tail plant to hold the contraption together. A long fork at the other end served as handgrips and a crosspiece held the harness.

Mooloolah looked on in wonder. When he saw Archie put ropes over his shoulder attached to the plow and Bonney guiding it as Archie pulled the plow through the soil he was so shocked he squatted down. He wondered how he could explain to these weird ones that all this effort to get food was a waste; was not needed. In the light of his reality, it was very stupid.

They became a constant source of amusement and wonder for him as the years went past. He learnt not to try to understand why they were there or why it was that the ancient families of the Kumbaingeri would be gone from their lands. It was a thing too immense to think about.

Old Mooloolah lived with them, or more accurately, about them, for nearly three years before the ancestors came to take him away. By then he had seen more change than his tribe had seen in thousands of years.

Mooloolah was buried near the tree he had been born under. He was honestly mourned by Archie and Bonney.

As they walked back to the house the old black had helped them build Archie said, "Ya know Bonney, it's a mighty funny thing but a man feels like 'e's lost 'is best mate."

" Right fine bloke 'e was an' I'm gonna miss 'im bad, Archie. Now who'll I 'ave t' talk to wen you goes off gallivantin' about?"

"You'll 'ave the nipper t' talk to by then." He said, giving her protruding tummy a gentle tap.

There were skiffs and rowboats on the river now, traded from the skippers of the Coasters for timber. The river was the artery of change, the safest and quickest way to travel.

From one end of the valley to the other the forest rang with the shouts of men and bullockies, the ring of the axe and the rasp of saws. The landing at the Big Bend was much used by the timber getters and the squatters, as well as the skippers, all in need of fresh food.

The 'George Sorrel' skippered by the inimitable Captain Smollet, sailed up to the Bend with Hay and Bert on board. Shifting bars in heavy weather seemed to be a piece of cake to Captain Smollet. His advice to the other skippers was simple. "Yrr need the Good Lord on the helm when you put yrr craft over a bar!"

At the Big Bend he ordered the sheet anchor dropped so Hay and Bert could go to deliver a cheque from the mill in Port for the first loads of cedar Archie had sent down.

Mister Greer rang the ship's bell vigorously as they rowed ashore. They could see smoke rising slowly from the river-stone chimney and Bonney standing at the door wiping her hands on her apron. They could not hear Hayward Bertram Conners gurgling in the split hollow log that was his crib.

As the white man sees it, Big Bend flat was looking good. Most of the trees, except those about the billabong, river and creek were either felled or ringbarked. Between the windrows the crops of grain and vegetables were burgeoning with life.

Bert and Hay went up the rise to the house. Bonney had their namesake in her arms.

"That's Hayward Bert Conners yer lookin' at! Ain't 'e a bruiser? Good t' see ya. 'Old on I'll tickle the bell f'r the old man." She went to the bit of iron hanging off the roof poles and gave it a 'tickle' with an axe.

The two men were looking at the baby with embarrassment and discomfort. They felt obliged to acknowledge the small human in some way but were at a loss to know how.

They were relieved when Bonney put him back in the crib and said, "Come in, f'r God's sake. Sit yer down an' I'll make a cuppa."

"Yeah, goodoh," they said.

They had had a cuppa and were lighting their pipes when Archie walked in wearing the baggiest and grubbiest pants in the north. Over it hung a dirty singlet full of holes. His beard looked as though it had been caught in a threshing machine.

"Goin' to introduce me t' these 'ere toffs?" he asked Bonney. "All done up like a sore toe. Never seen such a pretty sight."

The two dandies jumped to their feet and grasped his gnarled hands.

"Been all the way t' Sydney this time. Got all clobbered out with the latest. Archie, you should see it now! God's Streuth I hardly recognized the place. This place looks beaut, but specially the missus" Hay winked at her.

"The bloody missus! Look wot she been an' gawn an' done t' me! Made a man inta a bloomin' father! Never be the same agin'. Wot yer reckon about our boy eh? Named after youse 'e is!"

"'E's a beaut 'e is. An' the crops?"

"Crops! Ya seed nothin' like it in all your born days. The corn got up eight feet 'igh. Yer know, I bagged 100 bushel an acre! The oats got up t' six feet an' 'eaded at 18 inches it did. Wheat went rusty but. The veggies is grand. I'll give yous one o' me cauliflowers wen yer go. One of 'em weighed in at 36 pound! 'Ow about that then?"

"Yer know, we're doin' so pretty I can't get it inta me 'ead." Bonney confessed. "They comes in 'ere after tucker an offers us all sorts o' things. We got a milch cow, goats, a bullock, an' a tin with real money in it to boot. Marvelous ain't it?"

"Is that all? I've got a surprise f'r yers both. Take a look at this," said Bert, taking a large manila envelope from his pocket and handing it to her.

"Wots this then?" she asked.

'Well open the bloody thing an' see f'r yerself."

"No. 'Ere Archie, you open it."

He tore the flap and took out a piece of paper.

"Is this one ov them cheque things?"

"That's wot it be Archie."

"Wot, f'r me?"

"That's your name there ain't it?"

"Oh my Gawd!" He sat down heavily. His hands shook as he handed it to Bonney.

She looked at it and screeched.

"There's an eight an' two noughts! It couldn't be right! We only sent a bit of our cedar down!"

"Top price this season! Too right it's right. You're rich you two! Wot now?"

"'ome! I'll be able t' go 'ome!" Archie said.

A TRAIN OF EVENTS

When traveling by train I book a window seat in car A. Car A is the sleeping car that seats three to the compartment during the day. Sometimes if you get lucky you might have it to yourself some of the trip and I wondered if I would be this lucky when the train began the journey.

At the first stop, two old women reeking of cheap perfume got into my compartment. They had voices like hinges on a rusty iron gate. One said everything twice when she didn't say it more often.

" Arh, we are all comfy now Mavis."

"All comfy now Joyce. All comfy now. Been a good mornin though, ay? Been a good mornin so far Joyce, ay? Yairs. Very nice mornin. Good boy that Brian. I think Brian is a fine boy Joyce. A nice lad if you ask me. Very nice boy that Brian"... etc.

I escaped to another compartment only to be ear bashed by the occupant about the state of the world and how he could fix it. The old women were a better fate so I went back, breathed as lightly as I could and gazed grumpily out the window. I wondered about their long life during maybe two world wars, certainly the Depression, World War 11 and the radical social changes that followed. I dreamed of surreptitiously tapping into the memory bank of the tough old woman with a face like a plowed paddock sitting next to me reading a Barbara Taylor Bradford romance.

I thought how fascinating it would be to explore her mind from the inside. I lightened up. If you can't beat 'em join 'em.

"Going far?" I asked. It was the beginnings of a beautiful friendship.

They were in their eighties, old barmaids born and bred in Redfern, friends since childhood. I could see the ghost of youthful beauty and vivacity on Joyce's face. Mavis had had a tougher life by the look of her. There were hints of strength and a grim humour on her weathered face. In her youth I guessed she would have looked – well – interesting. She was one of 15 children in a rented terrace at 2/6 a week. Some weeks they couldn't pay the rent. Breakfast was a slice of bread and dripping when things were tough and two slices when things were good. Joyce was one of six. They were the only surviving members of their families, husbands and all. Mavis was longing for a cigarette and kept a tab on how long it would be before they got there.

"Been a very good girl I av. Avnt ad a smoke all mornin. Avnt even ducked off inta the dunny fer a puff. Been a good girl I av."

Joyce's family lived in the pub and her uncle was a leading sly grog dealer. Her sister wrote a song about him to be sung to 'South of the Border down Mexico way,' so Joyce tuned up and sang it for me, sounding off pitch and rusty.

> *Some where in Redfern down Walker street way*
> *That's where you'll find Tibby Orrighi selling sly grog night and day,*
> *The coppers they told him sly grogging don't pay,*
> *They said it would get him 6 months in Long Bay.*
> *Now Digby and Tibby got boozed up one night,*
> *One stouched the other and they had a fight,*
> *At the end poor Tibby he was as crook as hell,*
> *And poor old Digby's head rang like a bell,*
> *But when they heard the coppers coming they were smart,*
> *By the time they arrived they had a two mile start.*

'Who'll buy my grog?' that's Tibby's cry,
'I get a tray on every sly!'

The two fretted all the way about the verses they couldn't re-call and kept coming up with fragments so this is all I could get down. The song was sung for years by the family and was popular during the war even to the Middle East because they taught it to the soldiers who came to the Sunshine Club they ran in the church hall during the war years.

Joyce explained the foreign name; "Granpa was an Itie see? Course, his lot wuz all RC's but us lot wuz all C of E. Don't know how it happened that way but there you are. You believe in prayer? I do. Never been a night wen I don't say me prayers".

"Yairs." Mavis said "No matter wot they say. I wuz number ten of us kids. All dead they are. All dead and buried. Dead and gone. Wen the Boss upstairs calls yer name youv ad it I say". – Eyes and index finger inclined upward- "Times up wen e calls yer name. As fer me I'm glad t be on the way out not on the way in. Appy t be on the way out. World's not like it ust t be". Her old eyes looked sadly into mine. "Gone t the dogs. Yairs. Never ad no trouble walkin about at night wen I was a girl but damned if I'd chance it these days. Terrible it is. Yairs. *We wuz appy then.*"

(A telling statement about our glitzy post-modern world from an old woman that had bread and dripping for breakfast and lived in a two up two down terrace with sixteen others.)

Joyce nodded sagely. "Yairs. We had a lot a fun when we wuz growing up. We'd all get together an sing songs an dance about and uncles and aunts an visitors would tell stories an there wuz lots of church outings an dances Friday an Saturday nights. That's where you met your Bert wasn't it Mavis?" Mavis, wist-fully, "Yairs..."

Then Joyce told the story about her dad who was woken up by a mate banging on the pub door at two in the morning de-manding he open up and supply him with a 'half and half' that is, a bottle of stout and one of beer to mix as a 'black and tan'. Her dad stuck his head out of the bed room window on the first floor and said,

'Stone the bloody crows! It's two a bloody clock in the bloody morning and you wake me up for a half and half!' He got the bed pan from under the bed and threw the contents out on the bloke, shouting,

'You want a half and half? Here cop this you bastard, half of it's mine and half is the missus's!'

We all laughed for minutes.

I heard stories of births and deaths, adventures and misadventures and how things used to be.

"My last sister died right across the table from me". Joyce said "She wus pretty crook towards the end an came an lived with us. Choked on a bit of T bone steak I cooked her. What could I do? The ambulance blokes couldn't do much for her either an she died in hospital. But they got it out. Too late though. She wus the last t go God bless her... O well ..."

She looked out the window at the crops under cultivation then turned to Mavis and said, pointing to the passing country,

"Look there, Mavis, remind you of anything?"

"Nar - why should it? Paddocks is all I can see. Paddocks an nothin but. Far as I can see."

"You've forgot. Just like we worked on when we wus in the bloody Land Army that country." Mavis looked again. "So it is. Wasn't that a beaut time though? War or no war. Made yer feel good pullin yer weight. Wasn't we healthy but? We wus 'appy then. Didn't we 'av a great time. War or no war."

"Who had the best time? You did. Had a bad name in town by the end of the month you did. No doubt about you Mavis." And she gave her a conspirational smile and a dig in the ribs with her elbow.

"Oh that!" Mavis said with a laugh and a wave of her hand and let the matter rest.

They took their Romances out of their bags and started to read. But not for long. They liked having an audience. Joyce put the book down and informed me,

"The RSL at Tweed Heads is beaut. Biggest in the State you know that? We go there Fridays an put a few bob in the pokies and down a few beers. You get a big plate of tucker there too. Got a good club in your town? We've been having a holiday on the Gold Coast. Every year we take a break up there. I live with me son now out Penrith way. Mavis still lives in town. Wish I did. I miss it but the house my son lives in is very modern. Got everything. Big place it is too. We don't see that much of each other most of the year though. Mavis wants me t come to 'er place but me son needs a elpin hand with the kids an all. His wife left him. Be good t be back in Redfern though."

I turned to Mavis and asked, "Don't tell me you still live in Redfern?

"Too right," she said, "Back there now. Took a while but Bert an me bought the old place. Took im years but e did it up beaut. Then e died an I'm the only one there now. That's why I reckon Joyce ere should come."

"What old place do you mean?" I asked.

"The old place we wus brought up in o course. I mean it's not like it used t be with the bathroom and proper kitchen an all. I wus born there in the front upstairs bedroom with the fireplace in an that's where I'm goin t die. Them old places wus built t last. It's good t be back. No place like ome ay?"

When they said I must be disappointed that they ruined my hope for an empty compartment I could honestly say that I was happy to share it with a couple of fair dinkum Aussie sheilas. They blushed with pleasure and laughed.

"Couple of silly old ducks more like!" They said. Twice.

NO PLACE LIKE IT

Cattle Creek 1953

The day came; old Joe could scarcely believe it. It took thirty five years, four months and eleven days. He was grateful that ladling the raw sugar off the walls of the centrifugal machines was a long time behind him. It was hot, noisy and sometimes dangerous. In the old days, the spindles tended to go berserk and the drums, heavy with raw sugar, would break the bearings and create havoc by letting their constrained energy loose.

In his years in the mill three of Joe's mates had been badly injured by flying drums. He gave it up when he turned fifty. Too hard. They gave him a cushy job in the lab assaying each farmer's samples for sugar content and hosing the mill floor with the big pressure hose and sweeping the crud off the floor with a broom four feet wide.

Thirty five years, four months and eleven days on the cane or in the mill. Life in the cane fields or the mill was all he knew. He and his wife, Dot, had lived all that time in a worker's cottage on the edge of town. The house had a latticed front veranda, four rooms and a skillion roof kitchen out back. When holiday time came around they piled the kids into the old Bedford and drove the one hundred and five miles to Mackay. One year they even went as far up the coast as Cairns.

Like all his kind Joe was a tough as an old Army boot. When he walked home from the mill, he put his grizzly old head under the tank tap, brushed his sparse hair back with his hands and went onto the veranda to sit on the sagging lounge chair brought back from the tip in Mackay.

"Home, love," he would shout through the fly screen door, whereupon Dot would get a bottle of FourX from the ice chest and bring it to him with the week-end paper it took them all week to read. With a sense of duty Joe would glance at the headlines and get to the sports pages as fast as he could. Saturday was the big day of the week if Joe was off-shift at the mill. Well up on the form from the racing pages, he and Dot would go down to the pub for a counter lunch. (Pie and peas 2/6, snags and veggies 5/6, mixed grill with all the trimmings, 9/6.) With the races blaring from the Little Nipper radio on the bar they would argue the possibilities with their neighbours and bet a few bob on the most likely. Then it was home for a snooze and maybe a bit of slap and tickle then a cuppa out on the veranda, a shower and a spruce-up, and down to the School of Arts hall for the Saturday night dance.

࿐

When the whistle blew the mill manager gave Joe a send-off. Some foremen, the lab staff and some of Joe's mates were there. There was the obligatory speech and well-wishes, cupcakes and lamingtons and a few cans of FourX. The manager gave Joe a Citizen watch fresh from Japan. Joe said thanks, shook his hand and hurried back to the workers' side of the table. Later when he and a few of the blokes were standing around magging, Joe looked up at the smoking chimney and the open layered floors of the mill, drank in the rich smell of hot molasses and said,

"Bloody hell, Mike, wots a bloke to do now e's out to pasture?"

"Well the first bloody thing to do is go to the Royal George for a piss-up is what I reckon a man should do. I'll drive ya. Got the ute the other side ov the tracks."

"You're on. But stop home for a tick on the way."

"Right O - let's go – you blokes coming down the Royal George?" he yelled as they disappeared between the cane trucks.

"Wetting the whistle down the pub with the blokes," he told Dot, "but I'll leave the loot with you, love, or the bastards will con me out of a big chunk of it. Give us a fiver and stoush the rest in the bicky tin. Well that's that," he said, looking up the walls. "Wots a bloke to do?"

"Learn to take it easy. You could get a big veggie garden' goin'. Raise racin' pigeons like your dad. Fred took up wood workin' and did real good at the markets remember. Get a few Greyhounds – something like that."

"Yeah, well, none ov them things tickles me fancy."

"Is that so? Well, you better find something that tickles yer fancy. I don't want ya hanging round the place like a bad smell."

"Yeah, well, I'm off. Wots fer tea?"

"Pork chops, cauly an pumpkin."

"Good on ya love. Might be a bit late. The blokes aim t get me pissed."

"I should be surprised? Go on! Shoo!" said Dot, giving him a whack with the fly swatter.

Impatient now, Mike tooted the horn.

❧

All the blokes at the Royal George were downing their first pot by the time Joe and Mike got there. They pushed their way through the bat-wing doors. The timber floor drummed with the sound of their hob-nailed boots. The blokes gathered around one end of the bar shouted,

"Come on Joe, we got one lined up for ya. Here, take a pew." Bert pushed a bar stool out with his foot. The commercial travellers, D of Ag blokes and Stock and Station Agents at the other end of the bar looked on with interest. It wasn't long before there was only one group at the bar.

"Old Joe here retired today, see," Mike volunteered, "so we are givin' the old coot a send-off"

Bill gave Joe a nudge that nearly knocked him off his perch.

"Come on Joe you're the cove with all the moola. Fork out that big pay envelope and shout the bar."

"Hard luck Bill. The missus collared the lot."

Joe didn't come down with the last shower.

"Gawd blimey, wouldn't yer know? Tight as a fishes arse you are."

"Yeah" said Joe, "an that's water tight," he held the fiver up. "She let me off with this, but. Call fer wot yer fancy"

The blokes gave a cheer, D of Ag blokes, Stock and Station Agents, the travellers, the lot.

The only one wearing a tie was an executive from the Colonial Sugar Refinery office in Sydney.

"Retired eh? Good for you" he said. "I will be too, this time next year. Wife and I will take a trip overseas, buy a place down the coast and maybe start a orchid nursery. What are your plans?"

"Plans? said Joe, "plans? Buggered if I know. It's a bit of a worry. The wife has a few ideas. I s'pose somethin' will turn up. I don't want t' lay idle and rust up like a busted wind mill."

Not really in the mood for conviviality, Joe announced that Dot had a little celebration of her own he should be at. This piece of misjudgement brought cat calls and ribald remarks from his mates. As he pushed through the doors, he heard Mike, a bit wounded, shout,

"Piss off then yer randy old rooster."

Dot was knitting a tea cosy and listening to Mrs Iggs and Mrs Arris on the radio, when she heard the little bell on the fly screen door tinkle. She looked up at the clock with surprise. Joe sauntered in, sat on the wicker chair and began to take his boots off.

"What's up? Got a belly ache? You're early."

"Yeah. I dunno. Just wasn't in the mood. Those silly bastards will feel the worse fer wear tomorra I'll warrant. Let's eat."

Dot said, "Right O. You set the table then." She went to the fuel stove that she had damped down an hour ago, put a Feltex mitt she had made from bits of carpet twenty years ago on each hand, and took the two plates of food to the table. Joe went to the pantry for the tomato sauce and mustard but stood pensively looking out the back door, then went back to the kitchen without them.

"All the tomorras'll be like a day off shift." he said.

"You can sleep in long as ya like now Joe, an' we can go visit Madge and Barny, how about that?"

"Yeah. Gotta go to town an fix up about the pension an that stuff. Go the day after tomorra, how's that?"

"Just think! We can mooch about town long as we like. Go to the flicks and the *CWA dinner an you can do some fishin'."

He heard, but his heart wasn't in it. He thought of missing the comradeship with the blokes at the mill, of not having an active role to play in the local life centred on growing and milling cane.

"I reckon I'm gonna miss the smell of molasses," he said wistfully. Dot frowned a worried frown, but said nothing.

*Country Women's Association

A few weeks later, after they had returned from Mackay, Dot met Floris outside the butcher shop. "How's Joe?" Floris asked, "things looking up?"

"Tell you the truth, I don't know what to do with him," Dot confessed. "I tell you, if he doesn't snap out of it I'll send him off to one of those mind doctors. I'm about at the end of me tether an' its only been a month or so. I must say 'e brightened up a bit in Mackay but as soon as we got 'ome he got a fit of the glums again....I don't know....I'm gettin' so I can't stand 'im moping around."

"Tell ya wot," Floris said, "tell 'im to flag one of the loco drivers down and take trips about – that'll git 'im out and about a bit."

"Now that's a good idea. I'll tell 'im."

Next day, when Joe heard the chuff, rattle and clank of a loco far away, he went through the blackened fields where the cane had recently been fired and cut. He rolled a fag and squatted bushman fashion by the tracks. Sounds told him that the loco with its long line of cane trucks was out there somewhere. At that part of the valley he knew that it had to come down this track to get to the mill. There were no other sounds. The teeming life that was once here, like the dense rain forest, was long gone. The intense sun filtered through the breaks in his straw hat. He took it off from time to time and wiped the sweat off his brow and the cloth headband of the hat and perched it loosely on top of his head. Mindlessly, he picked at a scab on the back of his hand. He intoned the only song he remembered from his childhood...

The Camptown race track's five miles long,
Doodah doodah
The Camptown race track's five miles long,
Oh doodah day.
Gonna run all night, gonna run all day,
I'll bet my money on the bobtail nag,
somebody bet on the bay.

The little loco, looking much like those illustrated in kid's story books, chuffed into sight.,

loaded with cane stalks right back to the last truck. He waved his hat as it got close.

"G'day Joe. Wotcha doin' out 'ere?"

"Mornin' Ben. How's about I come along fer a spell?

"Well, s'pose it'll be all right. Come on up then"

"Wots on?"

"Gotta go way out to the Lorenzini's t' pick up a new line. It's a long haul."

"OK. I'll stick with ya if it's OK, nothin' better to do."

"Right you are then. Wotcha been up to?"

"Nothin' much. Missus an' I been a few weeks in Mackay an' I've takin' up readin' books but I don't go much on it though. Reckon I might try me 'and at growin' a bit a corn. Wots the news with you blokes?"

"S'pose you 'eard they got a machine for cuttin' cane?"

"Go on!"

"Fact. It's breaks down and jams all the time, but they keep workin' at it."

"Pigs might fly."

"You reckon? Well mark my words, the day'll come w'en there wont be no more cuttin'. Did ya hear the Robinson's are selling up? ...Benedetto's cane got the highest assay so far. He'll do well this year f'r a change."

"How's the Thompson's goin'?"

"Lost a few acres to the grub."

Feeling much better now, Joe talked the only talk he knew.

Late that day they rumbled into the mill yard with a string of loaded trucks just as the Union Foremen was crossing the tracks to get to the barracks.

"What the bloody hell are you doing up there riding the plate Joe?"

"Aw Christ Fred, just out fer a bit ov a trip."

"Trip be damned. I spot you having your bit of a trip again and I'll have your guts for garters. You too Ben. You should have known better. I've got a good mind to report you. Jesus Christ! What got into you.?"

Joe trudged home in a black mood.

How'd it go?" Dot asked.

"It was bloody well all right until that bastard of a Union rep spotted me in the loco with Ben Gaites. Scared the shit outa Ben. That's the end ov them little jaunts – bloody hell!"

and he went to shove his head under the tank tap. Dot got the bottle of FourX.

❧

A week later Floris and Mavis called to see Dot for a cuppa and to discuss some CWA matters.

"How's Joe gettin' along now?" Floris wanted to know.

"Bad t' worse if you ask me, 'e's taken t hangin' around the pub lookin' fer some lay-about to drink with. He'll wind up another of them piss pots is my worry. Not like your George, Mavis – Bush fire Brigade, Cricket club, running a few head, garden an' all. I don't know why Joe is like a cart without the horse."

At a loss for an answer, Mavis said, "Thank God George is outa the house most times. The Kanaka is back in town."

"Is that right? Haven't seen old Oolo fer quite a spell"

When Joe got home he informed Dot that the Kanaka was back in town.

"Extra big cache this time by the look of it. Took a room in the pub even. Where he gits them nuggets from is anybodies guess. Funny none of the blokes have ever bin able t' track 'im back. 'Cause the silly bastards take their dogs an' as soon as they bark after a roo or whatever he gets wise to wot they're up to. No body ever found out where 'e goes. Funny thing, that..."

The next morning Joe told Dot, "Got a plan love. I'm gonna sit tight by the pub of nights and w'en Oolo books out, I'm gonna folla the big brown bastard an' find out where 'e gits all the gold from. I reckon it's a one-man job an I'm just the man ter do it. He's gotta go slow with that big pack on an pushin' 'is wheel barra. I'm off t' git a roll o corn beef an a few tins a Camp Pie and stuff."

150

"Now you listen t' me Joe Wilks. You'll do no such thing. Way out in the hills on yer own an the rainy season comin' on."

"Wot of it? I been bushed, buggered, and wet more times than you've 'ad breakfast. Wots the harm? Wot if I comes back with a pocket full o nuggets – ay? - wot then?"

" Of course, Oolo will welcome you with open arms and show you where to pan, won't 'e."

"Likely as not 'e wont even know I'm there. I'll mooch about an see wot 'e's up to an do the same on the quiet, an I'm smarter than 'im by a long shot. 'E's as thick as a brick. I'm cunnin' as a shit 'ouse rat."

"An Oolo might av some big rat traps. Well there's no stoppin' ya I can see. But if you're not back in a week or so I'll call in the cops an' that's that"

Joe went under the house and collected his pan and sieve, sand shoes, water bottle, billy can and ground sheet and started to roll his swag. He was a man with a purpose. There was a twinkle in his eyes for the first time since he had been given a wrist watch. Dot put a paper bag full of Anzacs by his swag.

"All set then?"

"Reckon so." He went to the kitchen table and slung the swag across his back and the sugar sack across his chest.

"Wots in this?" He asked.

"Anzacs."

"Good on ya love Best in the CWA. I'll munch 'em on the way", said Joe, emptying the biscuits into the billy can. "Toodelloo then."

"You take care now, ya daft old bugger. Got some string an wire an a roll a rope?"

"Yep. All set. Got a feelin' in me water that tonight's the night too, so it might be a while before I'm back. Give us a kiss then."

"I wish ya wasn't goin' Joe."

"No t' worry. See ya soon. I'll be right as rain. Anybody asks, tell em I've gone fishin'."

Dot stood at the fly screen door and watched him sneaking off into the night. He went by back lanes to the old stables behind the pub where he knew Oolo kept his wheel barrow and squatted in the shadows. It was a long wait, but after the pub had closed and everything was quiet a figure snuck out of the back door lugging a big box. He went into the stables but was out again in no time. Back to the pub he went, then back again with two bulging sugar bags on his back, then into the pub for another. Joe was getting exited. He knew that Oolo would go by lanes in any direction but the right one and then head for home. Oolo, the axle on the ancient wheel barrow well oiled, pushed it, piled high with supplies, out of the stables, stopped, looked about him. Then he pushed it, going slow, around the back of the stables and hid in the shadows. After a few detours and stopping in shadows the old Kanaka went back of the football ground and headed for the hills, around wash-aways, up stony creeks, around soaks and hills. It was the long way home. Joe couldn't always keep him in sight but the iron wheel of the overloaded barrow left marks it wasn't hard to see if you knew what to look for. Strong as an ox, Oolo pushed the barrow all night – except for a few spells when he had a smoke and took a few swigs from a flagon of McWilliam's cheap plonk, and then lay flat on his back for no more than a few minutes.

At sun-up he boiled the billy and for breakfast cut a few rounds off a corned roll. So did Joe, hiding in a patch of undergrowth, wishing he could sip tea from his enamel mug like Oolo. He munched on Anzacs instead. Then Oolo lay down and fell into a deep, but short, sleep. Before an

hour was up he was pushing his barrow again.

The going slowed up. Oolo was not only tired, but pushing up hill meant many rests. He wasn't as young as he used to be. He would lay down, pass out, be motionless for a half hour or so, get up and struggle on. Joe wished that he too, could be like that. He was feeling so tired he wasn't game to lay down. He marvelled at the old Kanaka's endurance. He began to see that his notion of following Oolo was a silly idea from the start. He tried hard, but couldn't give it up. Couldn't be far to go now, he told himself, with more hope than conviction. Then, suddenly, came one of the greatest surprises of his life. Before them was a steep gorge. Up north a waterfall cascaded down rocks into a creek at the bottom of the gorge. South east, it curved away into gullies. Joe watched amazed as Oolo carefully manoeuvred his barrow over a bridge made from ropes, woven palm leaves and bamboo strips. On the other side, Oolo untied two ropes from trees on each side of the bridge and gave the bridge a mighty tug. The ends of the ropes fell into the gully, then as Oolo rolled the bridge up they went through forks on trees on the other side and were pulled in after the bridge. The bridge was the only thing Oolo remembered learning from his grandfather before he was blackbirded as a boy from his island home in the south Pacific.

"Strike a bloody light! No ones gonna believe this!" Joe said to himself. "'E's smarter than a coat of paint. No wonder no one could ever track 'im back!"

Getting a mite smart himself, Joe realized that there must be a way down and up the other side so Oolo could re-rig the bridge, so he poked about until he found it. Cunning, like he said.

Once on the other side, he found the tracks of the wheelbarrow and within a half mile came to a beautiful little valley with a creek running through it, shadowed with bangalow palms, paper barks and cadajis. Gaudy parrikeets flashed through the trees, with magpies, king parrots, black cockatoos, finches and robins aplenty.

He could see Oolo's humpy with the empty barrow outside it on a rise by the creek. There was a patch of goosefoot, colonial cabbage and pumpkins fenced off from bandicoots and wallabies. Close by were a few young avocado and mango trees with a stand of bananas between them. Down the creek he could see a sluice by a cut-away bank and an exposed bit of hillside. Joe was busting to tell somebody. He waited and watched for over an hour but there was no movement about the humpy. Dead to the world, thought Joe, and no wonder.

He decided to move far down the creek and around the bend out of sight and try panning the gravel. Colour came up first time. Only a few bob's worth, but it thrilled him anyhow. Too tired and hungry to continue, Joe checked the wind and decided that it was safe to light a fire. A tin of Camp Pie, a chunk of bread, three mugs of tea and a fag and Joe, feeling that all was right with the world, lay on his ground sheet and slept for three hours.

He woke up excited. Down to the creek he went, moleskins rolled up and sand shoes off, looking for likely places where the heavier silt piles up. Before dark he had two small nuggets and a pinch of dust. Next day he was at it soon as it was light enough. More colour and a small nugget. It was ten o'clock by the Citizen watch before he knocked off for breakfast, and then it was back to panning without delay. By four o'clock he had a likely hundred quids worth of nuggets and a thimble of dust, all told.

"Bloody amazing! Woopidoo! Boy oh boy! Wait till the missus cops an eye full of this lot!"

Joe said to himself. "Who'd a thought it? Good ol Oolo."

The thought of Oolo startled him. Gold was up for grabs here. No claims had yet been staked. The difficulties, obligations and responsibilities, loomed large in his imagination.

"Bloody hell," he cursed. Thinking about what to do about Oolo, he went onto the ridge and followed it along to a spot above Oolo's place. All was quiet. Nothing had changed. There was no smoke rising from the chimney. The long handled shovel and mattock by the sluice were untouched.

His instincts told him that something was amiss. After thinking this way and that, Joe felt impelled to see what old Oolo was up to. Slowly, looking this way and that, he went down onto the flats and crept to Oolo's hut. The hatch by the side wall was propped open, so he took a peep in. The boxes and bags were on the table along with two flagons. He could not see Oolo. All was quiet, except for the buzz of blow flies. Joe squatted, looking about and wondering fast. Then he moved to the other side of the hatch and took a look. No Oolo.

"Well, that beats all," Joe said to himself, "wot now?"

He crawled along the wall to the corner and saw that the door was open. He sidled along the front of the hut and looked in. Oolo lay along the wall under the hatch. Blowies were crawling out of his mouth, nose and ears. It had been one hard trip too many.

Joe's mind spun like a centrifugal machine off its bearings. What to do now? Tell everybody about Oolo and this place or tell nobody and take over where Oolo left off? Get a cache and cash it in and come back now and then to get more? Couldn't do that. Everyone would want to know how come he had so much spending money. Stake a claim so everyone could get to know and bugger the valley for good?

"Bloody hell!" he shouted out loud. Not looking at Oolo, Joe, dashing into the hut, grabbed a flagon and went and sat on the wheelbarrow. The possible implications of it all spun in his mind till he got dizzy. One possibility scared him. If he went back with lots of gold, maybe people would think that he had murdered Oolo to get it. The only thing Joe was sure of was that it wasn't decent to leave him to rot in the hut. With great sadness for the last of the Cattle Creek Kanakas, Joe dug a grave, dragged Oolo's body to the edge and rolled him into it, then went and got his swag.

That night he stayed in the hut, had more to eat and drink than for days, and poked amongst Oolo's things. He choked at the sight of some old photos of blackened cutters, wide, hooked blades in hand, standing by a horse-drawn tucker wagon, and one taken about 1910 of Oolo and his wife when they were young. A feeling rarely felt welled up inside him. He was shocked to find tears in his eyes. He found a Log Cabin tobacco tin so old that it was rusted about the rim and the picture of a cabin and man sitting outside the cabin smoking a pipe on the lid, was worn away in patches. Curious as to why a man would have such an old tin, he opened it to find it nearly full of little nuggets. He sat down and took more gulps of McWilliam's Tokay. Joe felt eerie and vaguely uncomfortable. He could look no further. He sat on the flitch, his mind in a fog.

He could not sleep on Oolo's bunk, so rolled his swag out on the floor and slept a sleep broken with strange dreams. It rained heavily that night. By morning the slab bark roof leaked and drops of water on his face woke him. He woke angry and irritable. He couldn't figure out what to do; what to tell and what not to tell; what to take and what to leave. The hammer action shot gun and bandoleer on the wall were a sore temptation, but he decided against it. Disgruntled, he pushed the hatch up and opened the door. The sun broke through the clouds, shining in millions of sparkles off the dew and rain drops hanging on the leaves. Magpies carolled, butcher birds sang their melodies, crows cawed and honey eaters trilled. It was lost on Joe, who spat.

Feeling like a sneak-thief, he raided Oolo's supplies. He took some eggs and bacon for his breakfast. He fried them in Oolo's frying pan, in Oolo's fireplace and ate them off Oolo's tin plate on Oolo's table, sitting on Oolo's flitch bench. Afterwards, he sat on Oolo's wheelbarrow with a mug of tea, smoking a fag in a fog of memories and apprehensions.

"Can't stand this place. It's too bloody spooky fer me. Bugger everything. I'm off home," he told the warming air. In twenty minutes by the Citizen watch, he was walking fast away from the hut towards the track.

On the outskirts of town, Joe hid his swag and sauntered into the main street. He looked at his watch. Six thirty. Good. Most of the blokes would be either at home or in the pub or rissole*

There were very few people about. He got home with a few waves, a nod and a g'day or two.

Dot had just put a pot of cabbage and pumpkin on the stove and was at the ice box for the chops when she heard the little bell on the fly screen door tinkle.

"It's me, love." Joe shouted as he opened the door.

"About time too. I was just on the verge of callin' in the cops. Where's your clobber?"

"Out by the dam. I'll fetch it w'en it gits dark."

"Wot's up Joe? You look crook."

"Crook's not the word fer it. More like up shit creek in a chicken wire canoe without a bloomin' paddle."

"Goodness me! That bad!"

"You wouldn't believe it. Sit down Dot. I gotta tell ya something."

After he had told her everything he put the old Log Cabin tin on the table.

"Take a gander at wots in it," he said, "it was the only thing of Oolo's I brought back. Unless I did, you would reckon I was telling ya tall stories."

They sat opposite each other looking at the gold. They found nothing to say. They said little during the meal. "I'll go fetch me swag" Joe said. He had done a lot of thinking on the way back, and as unused as he was to such an exercise, a few things started to become clear. When he got back home he sat on the back steps and mulled things over. He went inside. Dot was looking at the Women's Weekly but was too preoccupied with speculations to read.

Joe sat down on the wicker arm chair with a sigh. They sat looking vaguely at each other.

"S'pose you're onto wot this means then?" Joe asked.

"I don't know, it's all so confusin."

"Been thinkin' - all the way back. If we let on the cops'l git in the act an' will as likely charge me with murderin' old Oolo fer 'is gold. We can't suddenly start flashin' money around either. Far as I can see, either I take the tin back an try t' forget the whole episode, or we pull up stakes, move t' the big smoke, cash the loot in an do a bunk somewhere. New Zealand maybe, an start livin' it up there."

"What! Leave our home an town Joe? We can't do that."

"We'd aft t', don't ya see?"

"No I don't see. We've been 'appy ere all our lives. We belong 'ere Joe. If I can't live it up 'ere, I don't want t do it anywhere else an that's that. This is our home, Joe!"

"Gawd! All that moola. Think about it, love. We'd be rich. But not 'ere. If we stayed 'ere we'd be pestered t' death as to 'ow come we got all that gold. A bloke couldn't go fer a piss in the paddock without some coots sneekin' along behind 'im. If it weren't fer Oolo's bridge 'is valley would be full a blokes. There'd be a settlement there be now."

"Joe, you got a bit a gold by your own efforts, so w'y don't we keep that fer a rainy day, say ya found the tin out in the 'ills, an' give it all t' the 'ospital. Or the *rissole maybe, an we keep mum about poor ol Oolo and the valley."

"Now that's a good idea Dot. I'd be 'appy t' git rid ov the bloody tin an forgit the entire episode."

ॐ

So feeling greatly relieved, and busting with pride and self- importance, Joe and Dot went to see the mayor and tell him fibs about finding a tin full of nuggets, and reckoning it to be public property, to donate it to the run-down hospital. There were photos of them in the Mackay newspaper with the tin, and one of Joe shaking hands with the mayor, surrounded by members of the hospital board. Papers as far away as Cairns and Brisbane, ran the story.

When Joe woke up the next morning it came to him for the first time, in all its majesty, that he, Joe Wilks was the only person in the entire world who had been to Oolo's valley and knew the secrets it held. He knew things no other soul knew. He nurtured the secret as if it were a hidden treasure. Travellers asked after him and the locals said "There goes Joe Wilks," and pointed his home out to visitors.

A year later, when he heard that the old four bed hospital had new wards called the Joseph Wilk's Wing, he felt himself escalated to dizzy heights. Joe was a new man.

*Returned Soldier's League (RSL)

HOME IS WHERE THE WHEELS ARE

Gibb's River Road, Western Australia. 2001

Anthony Smart was a lecturer in Engineering, doggedly trying to climb the academic ladder. His wife, Millicent, was the very personal secretary to a leading industrialist. A childless marriage and high incomes allowed them to spend much money on items of social significance. He drove a Range Rover, she drove a BMW. The walls of their inner city apartment displayed paintings by up-and-coming artists, and one Dobell. They gave smart dinner parties where affairs of state and culture were discussed from the shallow knowledge obtained from TV and a hasty scanning of headlines.

It was understood that the bottles of wine brought by guests should cost at the very least, $25. A $70 or $80 bottle marked the guest as one of superior discrimination and intellect.

A recurring subject of conversation at these parties and lunches, was of touring and caravans, as Tony and Millicent were to do a round-Australia trip when Tony's sabbatical came up in a few months time.

The planning and talking about their trip was a leading subject for years. They brooded over maps and articles; which way to head first; south by the Ocean Road, west to the outback, north to the rainforest country and all the possibilities in between. Many maps had routes, long discussed, marked in red. The only direction they could not go was east. The desk in the spare room was covered in touring magazines and brochures about caravans.

Then the time came when the time had come to do some buying. Years of research and discussion had resulted in the elimination of inferiors and a tight matching of their needs and wants, which Tony had masterminded with the precision demanded by his profession.

With similar efficiency he rented a garage in the suburbs to stow the latest model caravan they had bought at a good price after some mock indecision and crafty haggling.

Millicent acquired the necessary 12 V television sets, radios, books and magazines, special clothing, sun creams, insect repellents, photographic equipment, and such like, until the only thing left to do was to make a final decision about what direction to take.

At the special and final dinner party, pieces of paper with the directions marked on them were placed into a hat and Millicent, on tip-toe and giggling, stretched up to pick one. She held it hidden in her hand and stood still, eyes closed. The guests held their breath. She looked. "West!" she cried. The guests whooped and proposed a toast. Tony, however, objected.

"As far as I am concerned, any decision a person makes should be based on an astute analysis of data and not on chance. I would rather go south"

"That," said Millicent, "is based on the sound data of one of your whims and nothing more. Why not west? We could go to Broken Hill and down into South Australia, up the red centre to Darwin and we could visit the Rock on the way."

If Millicent wished to tell the truth, which was the one luxury she denied herself, she would have to admit that as desirable as the adventure was, being cooped up with her husband day after day took a lot of the glow out of the prospect.

Experts in compromise, they went north.

Millicent wanted to go by the inland route, so she could see the New England country, Tony wanted to go by the Pacific Highway, so he could do some surfing. With superior reasoning based upon an analysis of data, they consulted maps, found the red Texta and went via the Pacific Highway to Grafton, then west to the inland route, then north to Toowoomba, over to the coast and then up to Cairns.

By the time they got to Mackay, each one was saying little, following their own internal agendas. The data, according to Tony, was the intention to drive around Australia. The intention according to Millicent was to meet people, see new things, explore, bush walk, and take pictures of their trip. An uneasy truce was the best they could do.

When they were in a caravan park, Millicent would start talking to people, while Tony was rather reserved. He interrupted the talk of whither from and whither to interspersed with delicious bits of personal revelations, that Millicent was enjoying, with information that it was time for the news, dinner, or whatever. When in adjoining shower blocks he could hear his wife chatting away to some stranger on the other side of the vented partition.

"Damn it!" he would curse, "can't even take a bloody shower."

When Tony started playing tapes of his lectures as they drove through the rainforest at Port Stephens, Millicent stifled a scream. When Millicent started playing a CD of Rachmaninov's Piano Concerto number two, which she considered excellent accompaniment to the scenery, Tony spat out the window and looked glum.

By the time they got to Cairns, various more-or-less satisfactory strategies had evolved. Millicent bought an Ipod with hi-fi earphones and had her classics loaded into it. While Tony listened to whatever, she would turn the volume up to max and enjoy the scenery.

Sometimes she did stints at the wheel when Tony needed a break, though it made him feel uncomfortable. Towing a van in a heavy four wheel drive was a job best left to a man.

By the time they got to the Western Australian border, Millicent was getting a bit sick of watching what she considered as dreary country going by hour after hour.

By the time they got to the Gibb's River road, heading for Broome, Millicent was getting tired of the whole thing. She decided to spend more time in the van watching TV or reading. Tony considered it be a good idea. He could turn the volume up and smoked as much as he liked.

One morning, not long after they had started driving, Millicent tapped Tony on the arm and said, "Never seen such boring country. I think I'll get into the van."

"Whatever you say. I'll pull over. I'll give you a call when we get near a roadhouse. Got your mobile with you?"

"It's in the van. See you."

Millicent got out at the roadhouse and took a turn in the cab the rest of the day, earphones on and eyes closed. The next morning, she opted to stay in the van. She was not feeling well. She thought that maybe the change of water, or the take-away meal of the night before might be the cause. Tony welcomed another day's driving on his own with the sound up full blast. Hours later he turned the radio on for the midday news, then pulled over to stretch his legs and have a piss. Millicent felt the rumble as the van rolled onto the gravel and knew that her husband had stopped for a break, so she grabbed a roll of toilet paper and made a dash for the scrub. Tony strolled down the road, counting the beer cans, drink cartons and cigarette packs, had a piss and drove on.

Deep in the dismal grey scrub Millicent heard her home start to move towards Broome. In a panic, she shoved the toilet roll into the pocket of her dressing gown and fought her way through the scrub back onto the road. She stood mindless as her home and husband moved inexorably westward. She stood in a daze, feeling the whole sorry plight to its depth and core. Images of reports of dire happenings, abductions, souls lost in wildernesses, and other stark possibilities surged up and took her attention up completely. She reeled. Feeling a collapse coming on, she squatted down and started to weep. The silence was abysmal. The dry heat, wide sky and scruffy scrub felt like malevolent presences coming to get her. She cried out to God for help, as all atheists of her kind do when in extremis. The merciless sun beat down upon her from a cloudless sky. She felt it burning into her scalp. She cried out. She fainted.

She woke to the dry heat, laying in the gravel, leaves, twigs and travellers' rubbish. She staggered to her feet, wanting water. Without conscious intention she started walking unsteadily westward. The thin soles of her fluffy slippers pushed the pebbles against her tender feet. She wailed a long slow wail. Far away, there was a noise coming down the road in the hot dry air. She stopped, turned around and listened. Something was coming. Over the crest of a far hill, she could see black blurs. A minute later she knew that it was a pack of motorcyclists. Once again she panicked. More grim images, stored away from long forgotten films, had brief re-runs. She forced her way into the scrub, hoping she had not been seen. Her heart surged down as she heard a bike stop. Others drove on.

"I tell ya, I saw a woman in a dressing gown and hair in curlers standing about here."

"So where is she now? You're hallucinating, as usual."

"Fair dinkum. I'll stake my life on it."

He got off his bike and took a look into the scrub.

"Yep, he said, "someone's been here."

He saw Millicent cringing down, eyes closed.

"Jesus bloody Christ! Look at this!" He called out. The others came and looked.

"What's an old tart doing on her own out here?" Then under his breath, "Maybe she's a loony."

One of the bikies said, "Ya make a good pair. I'm off".

"Look mum, is everything all right then?" one said.

Millicent whimpered, "Does it look like it, you oaf?"

"Well now, s'pose you tell us what you're doin' out here."

Millicent stood up, trying not to look too ridiculous. With a fine piece of editing she said,

"My husband is in a Range Rover towing a caravan up ahead. I got left behind."

The bikies grasped the situation instantly.

"No time to waste then. We'll catch 'im up."

He hitched his chains up and led Millicent to his Harley with the swept-back handlebars.

"Hop on!" He commanded.

Millicent hitched her dressing gown up over her knobbly knees and hopped on as best she could.

All the bikies had agreed that this trip was one of the best trips yet, but to the bikie with Millicent riding pillion it was an unsought event of some magnitude. He metamorphosed into a twenty-first century version of a black knight on a charger saving a damsel from distress and roared off down the road full throttle. Millicent gulped and wrapped her rose-patterned arms tighter about the bikie's solid black leather girth.

In the Range Rover, Tony was cruising along, singing to a CD of hits of the 1980's when a motor bike roared past. Unconsciously, his foot pressed down upon the accelerator, muttering *Bastards*. With a heightened roar, more bikes passed. Fifteen minutes later, he heard the familiar roar and his foot pressed harder on the go-pedal, but the bikie stayed level. Keeping his eyes on the road ahead, Tony wound the window down and gave the single finger gesture English Longbow archers used to frighten the enemy before launching a barrage of arrows. As the window went up he heard honking and shouting.

"Up you too, you bastards!" He shouted, as his foot pressed harder on the accelerator

Exulting, the bikie pushed his machine to the limit. Out of the corner of one eye, Tony saw the cyclist move slowly ahead. For the first time he got a good look at the bikie he was considering as an adversary. It appeared to be a large, leather-rigged, amply bearded, chain-bearing bikie on a Harley with swept-back handlebars with his wife, Millicent, riding pillion, shouting and waving at him, a stream of toilet paper flapping ribbons behind her.

In the ensuing second his mind analysed the available data. The following was considered in rapid succession. 1. As this was not possible, the experience must therefore be a dream. This was instantly deleted. 2. It must therefore be an hallucination. This was put into the pending file. 3. He had not taken an acid trip since 1974. 4. He had not smoked a reefer of heads since his affair with a student in 1982. 5. He was palpably awake and the experience, all data considered, must therefore be real. He got such a shock his mind went blank. As he rolled sidewards his foot came off the accelerator and the Range Rover plunged into the scrub, the caravan jack-knifing beside it.

Days later, Millicent, with a troupe of bikies, stood around a hospital bed that contained the distraught Tony, in the throes of hysteria. The nurse injected some more sedative.

The doctor informed Millicent that her husband was fit to travel and should be taken home and if the episodes of hysteria did not subside, that shock treatment might be indicated.

BOOK TWO

Dreamscapes

Like our dreams, these stories are strange, mystical, silly, weird, illogical, funny, whimsical, fantastic, poignant, sad, intriguing; or confusing.

This is in keeping with other strange writings, some by famous physicists -

'There are no divisions such as past, present and future, for they have contracted into a single moment where life quivers in its true sense...the past and the future are rolled up in this present moment.' D.T. Zusuki.

'For us believing physicists the distinction between past present and future is only an illusion...' Albert Einstein

In the words of his friend Robert Oppenheimer:

'If we ask for instance whether the position of the electron remains the same, we must say 'no', if we ask if the electron's position changes with time, we must say 'no'. If we ask whether the electron is at rest we must say 'no'. If we ask if it is in motion we must say 'no'.

And from an anonymous unfamous nonscientist:

' Logic and reason are the only things logical and reasonable in this world'

Because folk wisdom links vivid dreams to rich foods, each story is named after a food.

Bon appetit

Hearken young swain, I do beseech thee,
To this my council, that I might teach thee,
The things ye partake of as your foods,
Do caste the humours to diverse moods;
Distempers, wild imaginings, distorted thoughts,
Or dangerous dallyings with strange cohorts –
Methinks therefore tis but wise intent,
To forsake rich food as one retires,
If one be bent,
Upon a restful night of sleep.

Strange dreams and many vagrant moods,
Come to those who eat rich foods,
Before they hie them off to bed;
This by the very wise be said.
So caution they, being sore afraid,
That we are of such stuff as dreams are made

FRUIT CAKE AND A GLASS OF PORT

I am driving through a forest to visit a friend who lives on the mountain. It begins to rain in torrents.

A wind hits the tree tops. They lurch and thrash as it blows them about. Twigs and leaves batter the windscreen and fly past the windows. It is hard for my old eyes to see clearly through the pelting rain. There is a mighty crash as an immense branch breaks off a huge tree up ahead, crashing down among the smaller trees crushing the shrubs. Leaves, twigs and bits of bark are still falling as I drive past.

Getting to the open fields in the valley is a relief. I drive over the cattle grid onto the dirt road that leads to the house. Rivulets run by the roadside, cutting across it in places. I drive over the creek and see it frothing and bubbling over the stones. It is rising rapidly.

I sit with a mug of tea in front of me on the old plank table, nibbling on buttered toast, and look at the stove, black with age and glowing with heat, which rising, wafts the massed spider's webs about that hang in the gloom between the flue, walls and ceiling. The fire box crackles. Outside the wind catches a bit of corrugated iron and it clanks in rhythm with the gusts. There is a broken shutter somewhere. Rain clatters on the iron roof, so loudly he has to shout.

"Look, it's a bugger of a night. You should stay over."

We assemble the camp stretcher. He brings some army blankets circa 1940 and his granny's eiderdown.

"Should keep you warm enough" He says and goes to his room.

I strip down to my underwear, placing my folded clothes on the bench next to my wallet, glasses and keys. I feel quite snug under granny's eiderdown, listening to the rain drumming on the roof and the water gurgling in the down-pipes.

Then I was down at the pool wired against sharks, in the beautiful bay in Middle Harbour where I spent so much of my time in my youth. Only one house is visible by the cleft in the hill where the little creek runs between giant boulders onto a rock shelf before tinkling over the edge into the harbour.

It was night. I swam with slow rhythmic breast strokes in the dark water, little sparks of phosphorescence streaming from my hands. I rolled over onto my back, gently moving with small gyrations of my hands and feet until I felt my back touching the sands near the rock shelf at the base of the wooded hill. I lay there for a long time, listening to the lap of little waves. Up amongst the ghost gums an owl said "Mopoke. Mopoke." My body surged gently in the shallow currents. I was very happy.

I got such a shock to see her there. The day was warming up so they had come down for a swim. I didn't even know that she knew the pool was there, or that she lived hereabouts now, but there she was, bubbly as usual, her honeyed skin shinning like satin and the wayward curls bobbing about her beautiful face.

Confused by our mutual surprise, we said silly things to each other. After a while we were comforted by our old familiarity and sat close together on the bench between the rocks, our towels draped over our shoulders. I didn't think it strange at all that we were as we were fifty years before.

We chattered away, dazzled by the bright lights glinting off the ripples. The few little boats, white- spotted with seabird droppings, bobbed happily in the breeze. Everything took the spell. The glints bobbed happily off the water, the water bobbed up and down, the tops of the trees on the hillside bobbed back; even the dragonflies and the birds bobbed up and down as they flew. We were very happy.

The rain was still falling, but gently, murmuring on the roof, when she pulled the eiderdown aside and crept into my bed. She said nothing, but kissed me softly on the cheek and snuggled close. I turned and embraced her tenderly. We kissed, long and deep. The shutter was silent now, as was the sheet of iron. The silence seemed deeper because of the slow murmur of rain. I turned on my left side, knees up, as I usually do before sleep. She turned, her thighs under mine, her legs beside mine, her right arm over my back, fingers caressing my beard. We lay cupped together like two spoons, utterly contented. When the rain stopped there was absolute silence. I could hear her slow, contented breathing.

When I drove through the forest, the gusts of wind blew branches and twigs about as the storm raged down the valley. It was good to be young and carefree again.

HAM AND PICKLE SANDWICH

As the sun rose, the desert was deathly quiet. Usually, the only sound hereabouts is the wind, except perhaps, the barking of crocs of a night in the mangrove swamps. At dawn, somehow, the quietness was quieter, the shadows deeper, and strangely elongated. The insignia hung limp and still on the flagpole and the shadow of it reached almost to the huts.

Why they picked me to drive the huge overloaded Semi I don't know. Twenty three tons of it unloaded, but there it was. When I climbed the steps into the cab I had that certain feeling.

Sure, it was a bit of a fumble getting it all together to start with, but the fact is I did it with what I reckon was a minimum number of hiccups, grindings and shudders. I guess the others were too busy with their own problems to bother watching me.

It was a long time before I felt relaxed enough to think about other things. The challenge of being alone in the cab is to stay alert, with the constant roar of the engine under toned by the hypnotic burring of the 22 tyres on the macadam. The mind has a dangerous tendency to close down, though you stay awake. Sometimes the scenery is a help, but when there is nothing to see but desert there's not much to look at. All this is bad enough but when the road ahead is a straight black line with no traffic on it – well, you can imagine what it feels like hour after hour.

Others at the table missed the signals Evelyn flashed across at Bruce. Bruce either missed them as well or chose to ignore them – which is more likely.

"As far as Mother Nature is concerned she is definitely all for the sisterhood. As a man I feel hard done by. Children adore you, we men worship you – I ask you – how many sonnets and love songs have women written to men? Eh? A huge proportion of all manufactured goods are made for – guess who? Women! You women have been endowed by nature with all sorts of privileges so stop moaning. You have an enchanting shape and a beauty which can verge on the exquisite". He smiled a secret smile while he swilled brandy about in the balloon between cupped hands. The others were silent. They knew he was off on one of his tirades. They knew there was no stopping him.

"Still..." Liz muttered.

A Boeing 747 droned overhead, making for the airport a few suburbs away. Bruce took his time, listening to the love-birds chortling in the cage on the balcony, ill-lit in evening light.

"Consider the penis and the beard," he went on, "These two prove my point. They are Mother Nature's standing joke on the male gender. Who else but a jester would put this most sensitive piece of tubing and its attendant balls, which are even more sensitive, right there between the legs? I ask you! Within easy reach of small dogs, prickly plants and easily kickable by short women. The sensible place for them is tucked up in the armpits out of harms way. As far as I am concerned the fact that I am subjected to the indignity of hair growing out of my face is a joke and a lousy one at that. So we have to bear the tedious ritual of scraping it off each day or go around with a face like an Astrakhan coat." The others smiled wanly. Lyn tittered, slightly embarrassed. Evelyn looked up under her eyelids and squirmed. Roger said "Here here".

A Jumbo jet roaring aloft to 10000 metres, headed for Istanbul.

By nightfall I will be out of the desert and into the arid lands and the road will get to have a few bumps and curves in it, thank God. I tried listening to the radio but it didn't do much good. Only one station out here and it's crook. Of course, you get to thinking and maybe doing a few puzzles and remembering. You do a lot of remembering. Wondering too. Like, if I had done A instead of B when I had the choice what would have happened? Where would I be now? – Like that. I reckon there are definite crossroads in life where your entire future can go one way or the other but you haven't a clue it's a crossroad at the time. Like driving this rig. Once you set out on a road it's your life til you get there.

When you're rolling along and the road is flat and she's in the highest gear for the load and the light is good and the day fine, it can get to be peaceful sitting in the cab, dreaming away. You feel that every little part is doing its bit so the whole rig can roar along in harmony. It's a good feeling.

I am remembering that big crossroad when I collided with Lindy the second time and could have said sorry! And walked on. That would have been A. B would be me saying "We're making a habit of this. I'm getting to like it" - or other silly things. And that's what I did. I did the B thing and asked her to lunch and was round the corner and down the straight likkedy split. I might not be able to see the road up ahead, but I can see the sort of country it will go through. How was I to know? We never do at the crossroads. I can't reverse back and go down road A now, can I? None of us can rub out the past like it's a pencil drawing and draw another picture to suit ourselves like time is a sketch pad.

You dream a lot, sitting there, hour after hour. Remember and wonder, too.

Sounding like an aerial lawn mower, a 'plane sunk slowly earthward. The far-off rumble of a train gathering speed wormed its way down the streets from the tracks a kilometre away. It was getting late. Lyn and Roger had stayed back to help with the clearing away. Evelyn took her rings off and put them on the window sill so she could get her freckled hands beginning to show the signs of age, into rubber gloves. Bruce sat at the table still; quite drunk by now and well on the way to one of his bellicose moods.

"Bloody women!" He shouted. Evelyn said "Oh no! Not again!" Lyn said "He's off!" Roger said "You girls finish off. I'll go soothe the dragon". He put the tea-towel back on the rack and went into the dining room.

"What are those bloody women up to?" Bruce was lounging well back from the table out of reach of his brandy.

"Finishing the washing up."

"She's been bellyaching about needing a dishwasher would you believe! Bloody hell! The two of us is all and bloody Brian comes to stay once in a blue moon and she wants a bloody dishwasher. Where's my damn cigs?" He staggered to his feet. The chair slid back making a grating noise on the tiled floor.

On the road when you get to a cross road there's a sign – turn left or right or go straight ahead and you go to a named place and it tells you how far it is. Not like these dirt tracks we live on.

I might regret it now but I wanted him then and age didn't matter and that was that. I'm like that. That's me. You know? Might go for months, or maybe years, and not care much for anybody. Then I get a crush on someone; out of the blue it comes. It's not like I go hunting about wet between the legs or anything like that. I'm not the predatory female he said I was. Anyhow, it was up to him wasn't it? All I did was sort of bump into him sort of accidentally on purpose. He did all the rest. It was terrific though. Really really was. I was rapt I can tell you. Thought I had cracked the jackpot that time. I must tell you that I didn't know what love making was, before. He was so different. I suppose that's why I hung in there so long. I mean, don't get me wrong here will you? It wasn't all the orgasms and things like that. It was how he made me feel. Like I was everything. You know? A woman knows. He used to stay in me long after, just kissing and talking. No one else ever did that, so I knew. It was what made it so different. See, I was really turned on, eh? When I saw these groovy young hunks I got to wondering if I could find one like that that was as good and made me feel like that. You know? Young and spunky but like him. So when the chance came I took it didn't I? One thing led to another and it all got like out of hand. I wish I hadn't started. I really really do. I can't go back to square one and have another throw of dice now, can I? If I had left when I wanted to, before things got too wild, I wouldn't have got busted along with the others and maybe – just maybe – you never know – maybe I could have made it up with him. There's nothing saying that I can't write to him though, is there? And why not? Maybe he will come and visit me here. It would be real good to see a friendly face in this bloody hole. It's possible, ay? Anything's possible. Maybe we could even get together again, when I get out, who knows? Anyhow it won't hurt to write him will it? Maybe it's not too late, eh?

...You start talking to yourself too. That doesn't worry me. Lots of people do that if they're alone a lot. Instead of feeling you're doing something kooky it can get to be good fun. Like you take real people off and ramble on the way they do, or speak parts you sort of remember from old movies or books – that sort of thing. Anyhow I've had it right now so I'll pull over as soon as I can and stretch my legs and have a piss and maybe go for a bit of a wander. Caught myself dozing off a bit ago and it's time for a break. You've got to remember to have plenty of water and coffee and a bit of tucker in the cab before you get rolling. I always do.

The pilot in the Grumman was doing a circuit waiting to land. It was a beautiful clear night. The moon was near full and the river shone like a silver ribbon, its edges dark in patches or dotted with lights. Way to the east he could see that many of the tall buildings in the city were lit or their windows glinted in the moonlight. The great arc of the bridge curved black against the silvered water. Its beacon shone brightly.

Below him, in the cluttered maze of dark streets Evelyn Williams, wife of Bruce, ex CEO of the country's largest haulage company, well fed and acquisitive, lay snoring softly, most of the expensive covers kicked off. A loosely covered breast sagged gently on the matrass, the other flopped on top. By the bed was a glass of water and a pill. Out on the balcony Bruce Williams lay face up. His lifeless eyes, glazed in death, pointed straight up into the night sky. The Budgies sat on their perch with heads tucked under wings, sound asleep. A cat sniffed his bare toes, stared at the Budgies for a long time and slunk off. The coroner would find his copious dinner of fillet mignon, baked potatoes, Caesar salad, and two helpings of apple pie and ice cream marinating in a mix of coffee, wine and brandy in his ample stomach.

It took a few days, but the Search and Rescue team from Derby found the twisted wreck of the Semi at the bottom of a stony gully in the King Leopold Ranges. The spotter in the helicopter could see the crushed cab sticking out from the load of heavy pipes and the chassis trailer twisted and broken over a big boulder. "Who ever was driving that rig wouldn't have stood a chance," he said.

CURRY WITH MANGO PICKLE

'All this is honey to all this', the old man said, his honey-brown flesh shining from his outstretched arms. Up and over his head they went until his fluid fingers touched the leaves on the forest floor. His hands, still beautiful in their grace, swept down his body and arched toward the youth, Shvetaketu, sitting before him. 'All this is honey to all this', the old man said.

Shvetaketu, still as stone, waited and wondered. 'This is a strange teaching', he thought, 'What does he mean, *honey*'.

The old sage, Kapya, sat on his mat of Kusa grass, unseeing eyes half closed. When Shevaketu asked, 'Revered sir, what is honey?', no answer came.

Far away, in the depth of the jungle, peacocks called. Nearby, goat herders moved their flocks along, singing, tapping the ground or a goat's behind with their staffs. Boatmen striding back and forth, rowed their country boats against the flow, chanting mantras to Mother Ganga or singing fragments of love songs. The sweet odour of jasmine rose with the heat from below the forested hill. Aware of it all, Shvetaketu sat wondering.

Then, muttering 'Namaste Gurudev' Shvetaketu bowed. Wondering still, he walked towards the village. At the Kali temple he saw many bees, little dollops of pollen on their legs, flying straight into the jungle from the marigolds the Brahman's grew to make garlands for Kali, the Holy Mother. 'Let me think about this', he said to himself. He found shade beneath a Banyan tree, propped himself against the trunk and closed his eyes.

Far away, in the depth of the jungle, peacocks called. Near-by, goat herders moved their flocks along, singing, tapping the ground or a goat's behind with their staffs. Boatmen striding back and forth rowed their country boats against the flow, chanting mantras to Mother Ganga or singing fragments of love songs. The sweet odour of jasmine rose with the heat from below the forested hill. Aware of it all, Shvetaketu sat thinking about honey. 'Honey is golden brown, sticky and sweet to us, but what is it to bees? They hoard it as a miser does his wealth. Maybe honey is riches', he thought.

Early next day, as the cows were driven to pasture, Shvetake-tu went to Kapya, still sitting motionless on his Kusa grass mat. 'Gurudev, I understand that honey is riches but I do not under-stand your teaching.' he told the placid old man, who, smiling, said -

'This earth is the honey of all beings, and all beings are the honey of this earth. Likewise the bright immortal being who is in this earth and the bright, immortal being who is in the body are honey both. These four are but this Self. This un-derlying unity is the Great One. Knowing this is immortality and the means of becoming all.'

Shvetaketu wondered about this strange teaching a long time. Going back past the marigold garden, bees were buzzing about, busy as usual. Again he sat under the Banyan watching the buzzing about and the bee-line flights back to the hive. 'Such activity! So much work! How much they must love their honey.'

Far away, in the depth of the jungle, peacocks called. Near-by, goat herders moved their flocks along, singing, tapping the ground or a goats behind with their staffs. Boatmen striding back and forth, rowed their country boats against the flow, chanting mantras to Mother Ganga or singing fragments of love songs.

The sweet odour of jasmine rose with the heat from below the forested hill. As dedicated as hermits, the bees, never thinking of themselves, worked for each other, the Queen and the hive, without a stop.

Early next day, as the cows were driven to pasture, Shvetaketu went to Kapya, still sitting motionless on his Kusa grass mat. 'Gurudev, I understand that honey is love but I do not understand your teaching.' he told the placid old man, who said -

'This sun is the honey of all beings, and all beings are the honey of this sun. Likewise the bright immortal being who is in this sun and the bright, immortal being who is in the body are honey both. These four are but this Self. This underlying unity is the Great One. Knowing this is immortality and the means of becoming all.'

Shvetaketu wondered about this strange teaching a long time. Going back past the marigold garden, bees were buzzing about, busy as usual. Again he sat under the Banyan watching the buzzing about and the bee-line flights back to the hive. 'I will follow them' Shvetaketu said to himself. By the pond in the village he found the smallest puff of goose down and wetting it, stuck it on the end of a bee, dizzy with delight, legs laden with pollen. Flying not as fast as it would like, the bee made off for the hive, Shvetaketu running after, straight to the hive in an ancient tree, scaring the wild deer, the squirrels, the birds and ruining the aim of chameleons.

Cautiously he approached the hole the bees were in. To a guard bee at the entrance he bowed, saying, 'A little halt busy one. Please tell me, what is honey?' The bee buzzed in a grumpy fashion and said, ' What a silly question! Honey is everything! What is life without honey?'

Early next day, as the cows were driven to pasture, Shvetaketu went to Kapya, still sitting motionless on his Kusa grass mat.

'Gurudev, I understand that honey is life but I do not understand your teaching,' he told the old man, who said -

*'*This moon is the honey of all beings, and all beings are the honey of this moon. Likewise the bright immortal being who is in this moon and the bright, immortal being who is in the body are honey both. These four are but this Self. This underlying unity is the Great One. Knowing this is immortality and the means of becoming all.*'

Going home past the marigold garden Shvetaketu went into the jungle to the bee's hive where he asked for an interview with the Queen. 'Not possible.' said the drone on guard, 'Her Majesty never leaves Her chamber, but perhaps She will answer a question through me.'

'Thank you', said Shvetaketu, 'please ask her: what is honey?'

A little later the drone came back, (during his absence, Shvetaketu counted 753 bees bustling into the hive laden with marigold pollen). The drone said, ''Her Majesty said that honey is bees and bees are honey and that they are mutually interdependent One is the effect of the other.. Honey is the effect of bees and bees are the effect of honey.'

Early next day, as the cows were driven to pasture, Shvetaketu went to Kapya, still sitting motionless on his Kusa grass mat. 'Gurudev, I have gone to great lengths to understand about your honey doctrine - even consulting the Queen of the bees. She told me that honey is the effect of bees and that bees are the effect of honey and all is interdependent.'

' Just so!' Kapya said, 'they are one; the same though different. This is the mystery understood by the wise.

*Verily this Self is the King and Ruler of all beings. Just as the spokes of a chariot wheel are fixed in the nave and the felloe, so all beings, all the gods, all worlds, all organs and all these many creatures are all fixed in the Self.'

Far away, in the depth of the jungle, peacocks called. Nearby, goat herders moved their flocks along, singing, tapping the ground or a goat's behind with their staffs. Boatmen striding back and forth, rowed their country boats against the flow, chanting mantras to Mother Ganga or singing fragments of love songs. The sweet odour of jasmine rose with the heat from below the forested hill.

A small bud burst open, unseen, in a dark cleft of the gorge, becoming a glowing white star in the gloom. In the Ganga, a group of dolphins herded a school of fish against the bank with a noisy surge of water that frightened the ibis into flight. The temple elephant, sad and bored, tethered by a stout chain attached to a spike driven deep into rock, swayed slowly side to side, dreaming of freedom.

Deep in the jungle depths a tiger made a kill. Tired and panting, the tiger sat with its forepaws on the body of a buck. The westering sun, large and dusky red, shed its misty light on the radiant clouds floating over a distant land. About the village, the cows were being driven lazily home for milking.

In the temple the Brahman rang the big bell and began chanting the Gayatri Mantram - mystical sounds from before the beginning. Mothers put babies to the breast and elder sons lit the fires. Smoke drifted about the village and the smell of burning cowpats floated about with it – a smell the wild things knew well. As the light faded, birds went to roost and the creatures of the night sniffed the air to know the direction they should take. Silence as deep as the dark hung heavily in the warm air, made more intense by the short sudden hoot of an owl or the clucking of geckos.

Far away, a doe and buck were mating in an ancient ritual and some villagers in their huts were becoming amorous with each other. All home in the hive, the bees swarmed about the honey cells and the Queen laid more eggs.

Aware of it all, Kapya opened his eyes and said: 'All this is honey to all this.' Blissful, free and unafraid, he stretched out upon the leaves and with a contented sigh, slipped into sleep.

These quotes are adapted from Swami Nikhilananda's translation of the Brihadaranyaka Upanishad.

APPLE PIE

Last night I met The Perfect Woman! It was the last thing I expected when I went to the fencing class. I saw the advertisement announcing the start of the class in the local paper and thought it would be worth a try. I had always fancied myself as Robin Hood having it out with the Sheriff of Nottingham's henchmen and piercing them through right and left. Or maybe holding the whole garrison at bay single handed at the draw bridge. I was sure I would be a natural, so I noted the date and resolved to go. I know what I like and want to do and go for it.

I have always been a man of decided opinions, definite understandings, sensitive feelings and a clear idea of what I wanted out of life and how to get it. I am a no-nonsense sort of man you might say. Anything that didn't come up to my expectations or my standards I either discarded or avoided. After TM and Vipasana retreats, I now know that I have always been a man of decided opinions, definite understandings, sensitive feelings and a clear idea of what I wanted out of life and how to get it. I am a no-nonsense sort of man you might say. Anything that didn't come up to my expectations or my standards I either discarded or avoided.

After Rebirthing and Gestalt work, I know that I have always been a man of decided opinions, definite understandings, sensitive feelings and a clear idea of what I wanted out of life and how to get it. I am a no-nonsense sort of man you might say. Anything that didn't come up to my expectations or my standards I either discarded or avoided, When I was a Pre-Clear I recognized – or should I say, finally admitted, that I have always been a man of decided opinions, definite understandings, sensitive feelings and a clear idea of what I wanted out of life and how to get it. I am a no-nonsense sort of man you might say. Anything that didn't come up to my expectations or my standards I either discarded or avoided. But now that I am a Clear I see that all my opinions about myself have been a load of bullshit, to put it mildly. I now know for sure that everything I always knew for sure was ignorance, pure and simple. The worst sort of ignorance is not not-knowing, you know. The worst sort is knowing wrong.

Anyhow, being of clear opinions and definite understandings, with sensitive feelings and so wisely ignorant, I never married. Yes, flings there were aplenty, even a few D&M's. Though good women all (for one reason or another) none of them came up to my standards. Not so much that I wanted to marry them and do the death till we part, kids, kindy, school, mortgage and that sort of thing. The thought makes me shudder.

There were a lot of students in the hall when I got there. One so young that when he shaved up, he shaved down, was arranging us all into line. I was disappointed and unimpressed. I thought: what could this young shaver know about the ancient art of fencing? Then my world turned up side down. Into the group glided a superb female, undoubtedly of the opposite sex, who introduced herself as our teacher. I was surprised that the teacher was a woman and after some preliminary instruction she came up the line of us, all doing our lunges and wrist twist with imaginary epees. When the glorious creature came to me, she said in a warm, soft but deep voice "Ah! you are a natural – a little deeper now." When she came close and lunged along with me I saw how beautiful she was. She had the stature of a Greek Goddess, the looks of an angel, a mass of black curls like the Nubian Goddess Aphrodite, and skin as soft as a peach. Statuesque and beautifully proportioned, strong and confident but gentle, intelligent but soft and feminine, she was a miracle of a woman. She was altogether heavenly...

I said "Please do not come so close – you are too beautiful"

"Pay attention "she said, smiling a wistful smile that was entirely captivating. "Now follow me – lunge, riposte, lunge, riposte..."

"This is just like dancing." I said.

"Then let us dance." she said, taking me by both hands.

" But but but...here? With the whole class looking on?" I stammered.

"What of it? - Come..."

So I whizzed her off into a Steaming Fandango. The students didn't seem to notice as we sped up and down the hall as they were doing the lunge twist riposte thing. There wasn't any music but that didn't seem to matter one bit.

Soon the others were watching entranced, as we sashayed and pirouetted, waltzed and generally tripped the light fantastic up and down the room in a breathtaking display of spontaneous, synchronized, harmonious bodily interaction. I was aghast at the magic of it. It was almost unbelievable that we two people, who had never met before, were in such immediate and effortless harmony. The room became too small for us so out and down the corridor we went and out through the window and up into the night sky, leaving all the rest behind agog in a grey mist.

We stripped off as we went, our bodies drifting like autumn leaves back to the earth. Dressed in nothing but our lighter-than-light-bodies we were free to meld and did so, travelling together as one, far away, where we danced from star to star and swam nude in the Milky Way sipping the nectar as we swam. The Milky Way glistened with the light of the sun and moon which we could see glowing in the Stygian blackness of the dark world we had left behind. We told us we were free of it now and would never go back. With nothing but ourselves for company we had no need for any other, for there were no others. We were everything that ever was, is, or could be, on both sides of time or the inside and outside of space. We drank the cool glistening, delicious, silver light of the moon or the warm and golden nectar of the sun and needed no other thing to support our single body of joy.

We asked no questions of each other for there were no answers: or rather any question became it's own answer and so didn't need to be asked. The marvellous freedom of it fired other levels of our joy, almost too great to bear. It was just as well that we had left our bodies behind for they would have been burned up by it. A body can only stand so much.

Our favourite game was to ask impossible questions of the Universe and watch as it tried to find convincing answers – questions such as 'why do fish swim in water and birds fly in air and not the other way around?' or 'if two and two make four what do two and two make?' or 'why do people grow down when they grow up?' and such like. It really had the Universe stumped when we asked it 'what are you doing here?'

We can't say if this glorious life is forever seeing there is no time here, nor can we say it only began with our dance. It doesn't matter anyhow does it?

PHEASANT WITH GLAZED FRUIT

Being in London alone on a cold, wet, grey day in the middle of summer, I thought it very thoughtful of Her Majesty to phone asking me over for a romp with the Corgis and a cuppa.

Naturally I accepted the invite and politely inquired if I should ring at the gates or go round the back and what time would suit her best.

"Oh no!" she said, quite surprised, "I shall send a driver round to the Dorchester to pick you up. Shall we say three sharp? Excellent! Be on the curb."

Trying to brighten the old town up a bit, I donned my iridescent boxer shorts, Hawaiian shirt and best pair of thongs and stood in the drizzle on the curb just prior to the appointed time. On the dot, the Royal VW resplendent with insignias and flying a Union Jack above both mudguards, slid smoothly to a stop. The driver waved me back as I was about to get in, hurriedly came round the curb with his cap off and held against his chest. He was splendidly attired in jodhpurs, riding boots and spurs, long sleeved khaki shirt and old school tie. There were gilt epaulets on his shoulders. I was so taken aback I wasn't sure if I should have curtsied or not.

"Allow me," he said, opening the door and bowing. Well that settled that, so I got in, settled back and rolled a fag.

As thoughtful as ever, HM obviously instructed the driver to give me a mini sight-seeing tour of London town. Contentedly puffing away, I was driven sedately up the Tottenham Court road, did a circuit of Regent's Park, came down Baker Street along Bayswater Road and through Hyde Park into Piccadilly, down Regent's Street and then down the Mall to the Palace.

By the time I was ushered up the stairs I was famished, having skipped lunch in expectation of a right royal afternoon tea. As usual the Corgis were all over me in a most indecorous manner, considering the social status of their pack leader. After the obligatory romp with HM looking on with indulgent pleasure, we were called to tea. Charley and Phil called over and we all sat around the kitchen table as servants came in with the silver service and trays of food. As I said, I was hungry enough for two and was hoping for lashings of trimmed cucumber and peanut butter sandwiches, the marvellous palace fruit cake and HM's famous apple pie. What did I get? Pumpkin scones with cockies joy and a Narada tea bag in a mug! I reckon it was carrying thoughtfulness a bit too far but that's HM for you. I mean, you can't get to be the Q of E without knowing how to anticipate the needs of others, can you? I suppose, though, that it's too much to expect even Herself to hit the nail on the head every time. Anyway, we chattered away for a time about this and that until the real reason for the invite became obvious. My input was needed on a few points of protocol in a tricky situation that I am not at liberty to mention. Then Charley and his dad got into one of their differences of opinion about Canada's colonial history and its influence on the current French bid for seceding, and things got a bit heated up.

I thought that it was time to have a change of subject so I said in a contemplative tone of voice, "You know there is something mysterious about Sao biscuits." That brought the conversation to a stop as the three of them looked enquiringly at me, fascinated. "I cannot understand why they taste so good. After all, what are they but a dollop of dough, a bit of water and a pinch of salt? I wouldn't be surprised if they added some secret chemical that made them addictive so no one could just be content with eating one, seeing that Arnotts are now American owned." That started off a lively discussion I can tell you, and the contentious issues were forgotten, at least for a time, but with those two it wouldn't be for long.

Of course, I pretended to be overjoyed at receiving a real Aussie smoke-o after weeks of oat biscuits, water wafers and Twinings or Liptons in dainty cups with handles so small a man can't get a good grip on them. After we chattered for a while HM showed me through the rooms and halls she had recently redecorated, which I found rather boring but she seemed much taken with the projects.

Naturally, she asked me my opinion and if I would give her some constructive comments. After due consideration and as tactfully as I could, I pointed out that the carpet by the southern door of the dining hall was frayed and should be replaced. And that I really didn't think that having so many poker machines in the foyer was a good idea. I didn't mention the tea bags.

ALPHABET SOUP

The auditorium was packed with a motley crowd consisting of gaudily dressed students, all looking very serious and learned. They carried clip boards and had pencils behind their ears or breast pockets lined with coloured pens.

Aged intellectuals, many sucking on unlit pipes or chewing on cough lozenges and wearing well worn suits of grey or navy blue occupied the first row of seats.

Behind them were studious looking females of the academic species. They wore sensible shoes, practical slacks, eye glasses, little make-up and short hair; to a man.

There was also a scattering of public servants all dressed in suits of shiny black plastic with voluminous brief cases on their laps which they never opened.

Bearded academics, dressed with studied carelessness, and from various departments, eyed each other from a distance, or leant their leather- patched elbows on the chair-arms in attitudes of casual disdain.

The muted roar of learned conversation rolled around the group like the rumble of distant thunder, but came to a sudden stop when a strange creature carrying a sheaf of papers strode to the lectern like a warrior going into battle. Minus preliminaries, he launched into his presentation.

"It is my contention," he roared "That racial characteristics have nothing to do with the several cultures in Europe today. I intend to demonstrate beyond any shadow of a doubt that racial traits and tendencies and cultures are dominated and caused by one single factor!"

His neck arched forward as his blazing eyes challenged the entire audience, who sat transfixed. Pencils stayed behind ears. Coloured pens slept in pockets. Pipe and lozenge sucking happened no more. Fingers tightened on the tops of brief cases and elbows were removed from chair-arms.

A silence as deep as the deepest Pacific trench penetrated into their souls, the furniture, the walls, the ceiling, and up beyond the roof and down into the foundations. The strange creature appeared set in stone. A casual observer who had not been transfixed would think they were witnessing a tableau – at least until the strange creature took up his theme once again by leaping up and pointing a rigid arm and finger at his audience and shouting –

"But one single factor? What team has discovered this world-shattering idea? The answer is no team but me alone. It came to me in a dream, the details revealed in startling clarity!"

He paused again, hands upon the lectern, while he looked humbly down at his shoes, casually noting that while one was an expensive black brogue, the other was an old tennis shoe splattered with black stuff and badly scuffed.

"These details," he went on to say, in a rather depreciating manner, (probably the result of the shoes) "can only be revealed to those with a PhD in Linguistics and will be given at a convention that will be held later this month."

The students, intellectuals, academics, male and female, and public servants, looking agrieved, put away clip-boards, note pads, pens and pencils. They whispered to each other, looking cross.

"Why Linguistics?" the strange creature inquired. Everyone waited breathless. "Why? Because that is the clue to the revelation! I will show that it is the most frequently used sounds in each language that is the root cause of each culture. It is obvious enough when once revealed, but the read-out from my sensitive machines will provide the final proof later." At this he became almost ingratiatingly humble, saying in tones almost conspirational, "May I suggest that advance bookings with a ten percent deposit will be required and one of my assistants will be in the foyer to help you to secure your seat at the termination of this lecture." He stopped in mid-flight on account of an Orangutang had wandered in from the nearby jungle and was giving the ushers a great deal of trouble. Naturally, everyone's attention was taken up 100% by the commotion, much to the relief of 99.5% of the audience who were on the very verge of becoming bored. The Simian, who by the way, looked remarkably like the lecturer, was finally ejected, screaming abuse and invective at the whole proceedings. One might have thought such a happening would put a lecturer right off his or her stride, but the Simian on the podium merely looked patiently down at his sand shoe and waited. He was used to student riots and protest marches and the like. He stared for a time at the back wall. He was a master showman. An immense quiet entered the hall. He resumed in slow, well modulated tones –

"But for now, consider – the most common sound in Russian is Ch and Sh. You can tell a person is speaking Russian as soon as you hear ch and sh can't you? And what does this sound mean? They are highly revolutionary, romantic, slippery and mushy sounds and so are they. Consider French. It is full of ees and eecs and similar fine, expressive sounds which make them sensitive, artistic, philosophical, somewhat arrogant, and with a tendency to being conquered. Consider the German. It is full of ugs and aks and krs which sounds constantly produced, cause them to be excellent engineers, meticulous manufacturers, and of scientific and political bent with a tendency to wage war at the drop of a slide rule. If they all gave it up and spoke English they would all be like us in no time.

"Consider the Indian speech full of rolling r's and full round sounds and sibilant shss and what would you expect? Adaptability, religious manias, artistic softness and a compensatory liking for chillies." He stood quite still, looked intently at the middle distance, waiting until his audience were equally intent, gathered into one by the sudden silence. "Sound is more important than meaning!" he roared. More dramatic silence. "Sound *is* meaning!"

At this critical point, just as he was about to administer the *coup de gras* as it were, pelting rain began. Everyone scuttled off to the gazebos and boatsheds which dotted the landscape as far as the eye could see.

Through the bustle and the sound of rain hissing on the water, the sound of his voice trailed away, "Consider the urgent trilling of an alarm clock...."

STICKY DATE PUDDING

"I've been here before" I said to her. "This place is strangely familiar. I could swear that I know it in detail." I looked about the old market square – the cobbled streets, the strange old buildings now Heritage listed, the light poles to take the flares, the ornate decorations and gargoyles on the colourful buildings.

"Funny isn't it, how these notions can come to you sometimes? Not possible though, is it? This is the first time I have ever set foot in this country. In Europe in fact. For you it is different."

"I worry about you sometimes. The strangest ideas you get!"

"Hmm - well this doesn't feel like a mere dream to me. You see that ornate old building with the big arch door? I reckon that if you check it out you will find an inscription between two hour glasses, carved into the stone above the door. I feel sure it is there."

"Oh dear, Oh dear. Give it up wont you?"

"Why? let's go over and explode the myth. Come on, you've got nothing to lose except your delusions."

She laughed,"you leave my delusions alone!"

"Come on; be prepared to get a surprise."

We did get a huge surprise to find out I was right. She said. "Come on now! You sneaky thing. You've read the tourist brochure, haven't you?"

"Not guilty. Have you seen me studying them yet?"

"No, that's true, but you might have done it behind my back."

"Look, I tell you what. I am sure that I can tell you what it is like inside."

"Here we go again" She said.

I closed my eyes and just verbalised what ever pictures came up.

"There is a small foyer inside this door. There are big pictures of dignitaries on the walls, Mayors and Burgomasters and that sort of thing. There is a reception table. Two benches line the side walls. Then there is another big door but this one is halved and the two sides are covered in shining brass studs. The doors have huge metal handles that look as though they have been moulded to simulate the hind legs of a stag – something like that. Beyond the doors is a small auditorium I would call it. Maybe it's a theatre. There is a sort of stage, I suppose you would call it, and there are heavy silver drapes hanging off it and down the sides. On each side up high are two statuettes of women holding things like urns with grapes and fruit spilling out. Now it is getting packed. I hear a gun shot. A man in the box seat falls over. There is great consternation. I don't want to do this anymore!"

I opened my eyes with great relief that all this was not now. We looked at each other in silence.

After a long time she said. "You did that so well I almost believed it."

"I believe it. Let's go in."

The big door swung open to reveal the foyer just as I had predicted. She was aghast with incredulity.

"My God!" I croaked, "It's just as I said it would be! There are the swinging doors with the strange handles too. Now for the next bit!" I was very excited by this time, so much so that I wasn't exactly me. Well, what I mean is I was still the same me, but I didn't look like me. I felt fat and proud and pompous and wore a huge wig of all things, and waddled as I walked and a sword dangled from the many buckled belt about my bulging belly.

She grabbed my arm. "Josh, don't. I don't want to go in. I've had enough for one day." That brought me back.

I tried the door but it was locked.

"Look – there's a notice on the door. I wonder what it says"

It was then that a man in some sort of uniform came up to us. I asked him, "What does the inscription over the door mean?"

In broken English he said "Over the door is carved 'Time is of the Essence' but I don't know what it means"

"Thank you. What does this notice on the door say?"

"Notices don't *say* anything" Rather surprised at his reply I tried again.

"What does this notice read?"

"Mine Gott! Notices can't *read* either." I was getting angry.

"Can you read?"

"Yar.."

"Then please read this notice for us."

"Yarvol. Notice is: *Public access to this building is forbidden until after the renovations are complete. The building is due to be opened in the third week of June 1882.*"

We have never mentioned this incident to another soul. We never speak of it.

Though it was broad daylight the traffic and window-shoppers were thinning out, so it was probably about One o'clock on Saturday. Pigeons were billing and cooing in the gutters and on the awnings overhead.

As we stood on the footpath outside the shop front I said "I've been here before"

"You're always saying things like that" She said. She was getting irritable from all the walking about.

"Yes, deja vu is very big with me I know." 'Agree with thine adversary quickly' – I had learnt that one early in our relationship.

"Well, what's this one about?"

"It's about a memorable day twenty years ago. This trendy Brasserie used to be the old Repin's coffee shop".

"Whatever it used to be, right now it's a place we can sit for a while and have a snack and a glass of vino."

"If that's what you want. I don't mind."

Inside this now up-market hostelry the chairs were covered in black plastic to look like leather. Imitation brass railings and fittings were a big feature. There were imitation brass candelabras on each table, each one topped with an imitation flame.

A young waitress took our order. She was dressed all in black – blouse, shirt, stockings, and shoes – all in the same shade of black.

Everything went black.

"I've been here before" I said to her. "This is the hang-out, the home-away-from, the roost. We all get together upstairs. It's got the best coffee in town."

It was good to get back and smell the aroma of percolating coffee dripping slowly down into the big Pyrex jugs on the warming pads.

The friendly tan wooden cubicles, separate and private, lined the walls. Waitresses patrolling with the coffee jugs kept the customer's cups topped up or carried plates of food on trays. They wore little caps and aprons and looked very homely.

"Gday Bette," "Morning Flo" "Looking good, Eva". They all gave me a welcome smile. This surprised her a little and she gave me a quizzical look.

Upstairs the front cubicles were by the big windows looking out onto the street. You could look out and see the people on the footpath opposite and the pigeons perched on the window sills and ledges of the buildings. In the middle of the room were tables and chairs.

Sometimes it seemed that the only good thing in life was to sit here with Les, Harvey and Tom or whoever, talk and gaze down onto the world and the trams clattering past and drink endless cups of coffee.

That was the day Dennis decided to lunch here instead of the corner pub down from the Bulletin office. It also happened to be the day most of the blokes turned up. Serendipity? Synchronicity? Who knows? It just happened that way.

We all spotted the difference in Dennis straight away. Something had definitely happened to him so we all wondered to ourselves, what it must have been. It was a puzzlement, so when he called us over to his table we went. He was unusually dressed. He had left his grubby old Harris Tweed sports coat with the fob pocket and leather trimmed cuffs at home – or whereever home was the night before. He wore an old yachting jacket instead. His shirt was clean, his tie straight, his hair and beard trimmed, his jacket did not look as if he had slept in it for a week and his nails were clean. Not the least surprising thing about Dennis that day was his affability. There were no snide remarks or biting criticism directed to anybody – not even the church, Menzies or Liz. The great Dennis was holding court again.

"Gentlemen, I give you good day," he said, smiling. (There was often something a bit pompous and affected in Dennis which we supposed to be a hangover from his classical education at some august English temple of learning.)

"Rather splendid one, is it not? Very special one for me you know – having a sort of celebration. I have this very morn decided that it is time to change my ways; pull the socks up, turn over a new leaf and all that sort of stuff. Having a bit of good company and a hearty lunch." We were all fascinated by this unexpected declaration and pulling our chairs up, sat down. We watched mystified as he ordered his lunch of roast leg of lamb with roast vegetables and minted peas with the best of manners. He did not take swigs of booze from a flask as he usually did when away from a pub. It was all very suspicious. One does not like to give up the myths and legends built up about famous ratbags like Dennis. Stories about his misadventures and misdemeanours were legion. I supposed, then, that this incident would be another. I didn't know how right I was.

We ordered our toasts or whatever the budget could run to and listened to Sydney's most infamous Bohemian while we munched on whatever it was.

"There's a lot of worthwhile reading in the Good Book you know – or so I have been told. 'Go to the ants ye sluggards' and 'Get ye behind me Satan'. The further behind the better, I should say. I found a copy in the hotel room I wound up in last night and got to reading it for a while. Some of it is almost as good as Shakespeare for pithy prose and poetry. I recommend it to you."

This was going from the mysterious to the unbelievable. We looked at each other in stunned wonder.

"But for all time as for today, it is the Old Persian for me. Good old Omar. It bides you well, young chaps, to lend an ear to old Omar. Consider:

'The worldly hope men set their hearts upon,
Turn ashes, or they prosper, and anon,
Like snow upon the desert's dusty face,
Light but a lonely hour – and are gone!'

True. Too true. And this.

'Tis all a chequer board of nights and days,
Where Fate with men for pieces plays,
And shifts and moves,
And one by one,
Back in the closet lays'

He pondered these quotes intently as he finished his meal and pushed the plate to one side.

"Now for a jolly old smoke - but you should know that this is the last time I load the old briar. Giving up the smelly habit as of today." Our wonder deepened even further. Silently he packed his pipe, struck a match and puffed away in the most contented manner, leaning back away from the table and surveying us with a look that could only be described as benign. What ever was going on, I wondered. Because I was sitting opposite him, I accidentally caught his eye. He smiled at me and winked! This was doubly disconcerting because I was often the subject of his distemper. The situation was now getting eerie

"I've straightened everything up. Absolutely everything. There's not a loose end in sight. I've filed my piece with the Bulletin, corrected the proofs of the book, paid rent in arrears and all that sort of thing."

He smoked contentedly on as we sat saying little because we were too confused. A person acting so much out of character is very off-putting.

"Well chaps, that's it." He said. "Must be going."

He took from his jacket pocket a .22 Derringer, and putting the muzzle to the roof of his mouth, pulled the trigger.

I met Dennis again one week before I was killed when the old building I was renovating and restoring collapsed on top of me. Though he was only a baby I knew it was him. He was way up north somewhere. I think it was Norway. He looked at me (the eyes were new and just learning how to focus, but it was the old Dennis there behind them.) He said:

"I have been here before. I know this place. Maybe it's the remembrance of a dream, but I am sure I know it well. If I can describe the place to you, and I get it right, it must mean that I have been here before. There's a lot to it; too much to detail, so I'll just give you a general picture. The first and most impressive thing about this place is multiplicity and variety. That's one reason why there is too much to tell. The parts are so dissimilar that it's hard to believe that they belong to the same place. Basically it's flat, bumpy, hilly, mountainous, hot, cold, dry, wet, forested and bare and lots of it is nothing but sand, and all this is only the smallest part of it. Most of it is deep water. In spite of that they call it earth. It's a very strange place. This place is teeming with living things that eat each other and are only different sorts of tubes. Some of the tubes are so small that they can not be seen while some are so huge a human can pass through. Every one of these strange things have to constantly find the right bits of the world it lives in to put into its tube. It's very bizarre because most of it is lost through a hole at the other end of the tubes and goes back into the world again. A great strangeness is that because they can only see differences, they do not know that they are really cells in the same body. So everything they do and think is based on error. Error rules here. It's strangeness never ends. Everything here is borrowed; all the energy from light to food comes from another place. – how am I doing, getting it right? This place has nothing of its own. It is so weird that if it didn't exist, it could not be imagined. It is a mad house of begetting, becoming and death. This place is well lit most of the time but it really is a very dark place for it has no light of its own. Even the little sparks of light in its trillions of creatures is not part of it either. It has no substance at all, this place. It's a spectre on the mist; utterly weird and indescribably wonderful. It's where fallen angels come to suffer. I know this place well. I have been here lots of times. That's why I have to create a new literary form and invigorate the language of this country. You too."

He gave me a wink and a smile – exactly like the one he gave me in Repins all those years ago and said "See you later." Then he faded away into the dreamscape but his words lingered a long time. 'You too...See you later...'

Of course, I did not know then that before the week was out I would be laying dead under a pile of stone and ancient bricks. The arch over the doorway came down too and the stone into which was carved 'Time is of the Essence' was broken into fragments.

PLUM PUDDING

My first day at school is one of my clearest memories. We kids were told to form groups according to whatever religion we belonged to. I didn't know what I was. There was no religious indoctrination in our family. When the teacher called out 'Church Of England' I thought that must be my religion because mum and dad came from England. I was a daft kid. When I got home that first day mum asked me what I had learnt. I said not much – I have to go back tomorrow. But I don't remember that.

Memories are strange things. Of all the happenings in my crucial fifth year this is the only memory that comes back clear as glass. Everything else has been filtered out. There must be some significance in that.

So, once every week for years we went to the scripture class. I was very impressed with the minister because he looked a lot like Santa Claus. Maybe I thought that he had some special presents for me. I was impressed too by the Bible stories he told and by the illustrations on big canvas rolls in gaudy colours. I was very impressionable..

He taught us the Lord's Prayer of course. We were told never to go to bed without kneeling down and saying it with our palms together. We were to finish it by praying:

> If I should die before I wake,
> I pray the Lord my soul to take.

I said these prayers every night. Even mum and dad didn't know. It was my secret.

Being me, I did not say the prayer exactly as he wanted us to. My version was edited to accord with my private notions. Because I was being honest, I was sure the Lord would understand. Even approve. My prayer was:

Our Mother
(I had seen our cat and dog give birth and fathers didn't
seem to have anything to do with anything being here.
This made a lot of sense to me)
Who art everywhere and heaven too,
Hooray for your name,
Your Kingdom is coming
Your will be done
In earth as it is in heaven,
But not your wont.
Give us this day our daily meat, veggies and fruit,
(I didn't like bread)
And forgive us all for everything
because you are glorious and powerful. Amen.

Yes, I was very impressionable; somewhat strange perhaps. Certainly original. Then I would get into bed and say the dying prayer. I could catch a fleeting glimpse of oceans of light booming on oceans of power as I drifted through it into sleep. I thought that everyone went to sleep like that.

I used to sleep so deeply it was very difficult to awaken me. When the Jap submarines entered Sydney Harbour and sunk a ship and all the sirens went off, dad couldn't wake me. He carried me to the bathroom and ran cold water on my head before I woke up. We all sat like fools under the kitchen table covered with doonas and blankets and I went right back to sleep until I woke back in my bed next morning. That's all I know of the whole affair.

Years later, for reasons long forgotten, the family went to a church service. I was mightily impressed with the whole business; flowers, smells, altar, and the minister in robes playing to a packed house of people who put lots of money in a box his assistants brought around. My ambition was sealed. On the way home I confided to mum that I was going to be a minister when I grew up - but I would let her in for nothing.

When I was about thirteen I was sent to another school. Everything was different and I didn't like it. The boys were rude and tough and so were the teachers. The bullies gave me a hard time. One day one of the nastiest of them gave me a small box containing some pills. He held me by shirt collar and said,

'Here yar wimp. Wanna go t eaven? Try one of these. Go on - I dare ya. Go on or I'll belt you one'. I remembered the fat minister and the glories of heaven and not be be intimidated by the oaf said, 'Heaven eh? Sounds good to me. I'll take the lot!' And I did.

At first I seemed to be deeply asleep for a very long time, until shadows of people I had never met came floating about me. I was in some strange place I didn't like. The people said things that echoed and meant nothing. Mum and dad, my brother and sister drifted by and wafted off and came drifting by again. I thought maybe I had woken up when I saw a row of glistening beds going down a long corridor and heard strange sounds that rang hollow. Tiny figures from way down the corridor sped towards me and grew huge above me and then shrank away to nothing. Everything shimmered and came and went rapidly like sunlight on ripples. Then everything in the grey mist I was floating in became still and quiet. Then only the space into which everything went was left. There was only nothing.

. I began to move in it, flowing in an infinite ocean that had no top nor any bottom, towards to core of the worlds, where I became the earth and every smell, noses and thumbs, water and every taste, tongues and index fingers, air and every touch, skins and long fingers, fire and every sight, eyes and ring fingers, space and every sound, ears and little fingers. I held all the worlds in my hands, with their Gods; the twelve radiant ones, the eleven that shone, and the eight bright ones. Then I left all solids, liquids, gasses, light, and space behind. I went beyond the world for I had become its five-fold essence.

I heard these words, huge and hollow, boomed throughout all flows of time, from all beginnings to all endings, thens, nows and futures. The booming filled all space from there to here to far away, from all my years of saying them -

If I should die before I wake,
I pray the Lord my soul to take.

I don't know who it was, but whoever it was, he radiated nothing but pure, disinterested love and shone in silver and gold like nothing on earth could ever shine no matter how much power it consumed. Yet he was unassuming, humble and gentle. Being all love he had no need for any other power. His hands stretched out to me. His thumbs touched distant galaxies and his little fingers touched the beginnings and endings of the milky way. 'Come' he said.

An ethereal ship afloat upon an ethereal sea, blown slowly along by ancient winds, the spark of awareness floated through shimmering grey mists towards distant shadows of the rising moon.

The eternal spark, full of faculties, could see where it had been. The body lay disintegrating, the organs where the faculties once dwelt now empty and falling apart, useless. Joy burgeoned like spring buds.

I sailed the boisterous sea from whence spring all bodies and knew them all from one-celled amoebas to giant whales and elephants but wasted no time there. Then I sailed the sea of sparks, flowing in and out with the breathing of the universe, now out in the miracle of creation now in, in the miracle of annihilation. I loved it in joy, shock and wonder and looked forward to whatever sea was next because though it was unknown, I knew it would be sure to be another wonder. And it was.

I crossed the sea of sparks and sailed, blown by past winds, into the shining sea of mind, where every wave and ripple was a marvellous idea and pure creative knowledge shone with the splendour of a thousand suns.

Leaving the moon shadows behind, the quickening currents sped me through ever finer tissues of light where the radiant spirits dwell, to the cool, clear core of the sun, where the God of the Cosmos chants everything into seeming to be; where great souls dwell in timeless bliss and where nothing can disturb their infinite peace for there is no time here, as time has not yet begun for it has run its course. I know the freedom of ever-new joy. I can know all things, for I can be all things. I have no fear - even of ignorance. This, indeed, is heaven.